The Absolute

Even the book morphs!
Flip the pages
and check it out!

Look for other **ANIMORPHS**® titles by K.A. Applegate:

#1 The Invasion
#2 The Visitor
#3 The Encounter
#4 The Message
#5 The Predator
#6 The Capture
#7 The Stranger
#8 The Alien
#9 The Secret
#10 The Android
#11 The Forgotten
#12 The Reaction
#13 The Change
#14 The Unknown
#15 The Escape
#16 The Warning
#17 The Underground
#18 The Decision
#19 The Departure
#20 The Discovery
#21 The Threat
#22 The Solution
#23 The Pretender
#24 The Suspicion
#25 The Extreme
#26 The Attack
#27 The Exposed
#28 The Experiment
#29 The Sickness
#30 The Reunion
#31 The Conspiracy
#32 The Separation
#33 The Illusion

#34 The Prophecy
#35 The Proposal
#36 The Mutation
#37 The Weakness
#38 The Arrival
#39 The Hidden
#40 The Other
#41 The Familiar
#42 The Journey
#43 The Test
#44 The Unexpected
#45 The Revelation
#46 The Deception
#47 The Resistance
#48 The Return
#49 The Diversion
#50 The Ultimate

<MEGAMORPHS>
#1 The Andalite's Gift
#2 In the Time of Dinosaurs
#3 Elfangor's Secret
#4 Back to Before

The Hork-Bajir Chronicles
Visser
The Ellimist Chronicles

ALTERNAMORPHS
The First Journey
The Next Passage

The Absolute

K.A. Applegate

AN
APPLE
PAPERBACK

SCHOLASTIC INC.
New York Toronto London Auckland Sydney
Mexico City New Delhi Hong Kong

The author wishes to thank Lisa Harkrader
for her help in preparing this manuscript.

Thank you to Art Alphin

For Larry, Austin, and Ashley

And for Michael and Jake

Cover illustration by David B. Mattingly
Art Direction/Design by Karen Hudson/Ursula Albano

ISBN 0-439-11525-6

12 11 10 9 8 7 6 5 4 3 2 1   1 2 3 4 5 6/0

Printed in the U.S.A.
First Scholastic printing, March 2001

CHAPTER 1

I dove. Tucked my wings. Folded my tail. Hurtled toward earth!

I was a bullet. A bullet with feathers.

And feeling pretty righteous until Tobias rocketed past. He skimmed the top of the freight train and looped sideways in a corkscrew roll, wing over wing. His feathers grazed the big gun of one of the tanks.

<Show-off,> I said.

<Hey, I'm a hawk.> He pulled out of the roll. <I only get so many hobbies, and perfecting my Red-Tail Spiral of Death happens to be my favorite.>

We pumped our wings and shot past the loco-motive. Two guys wearing bib overalls and ball caps sat inside. One, the engineer, I guessed, was driving while the other watched the track ahead.

They weren't wielding Dracon beams. Or weapons of any kind. And they weren't paying any attention to the osprey and red-tailed hawk who'd dropped from the sky to spy on them.

<They don't *look* like Controllers,> said Tobias. <Like that means anything.>

<Yeah. Everything looks normal,> I said. <Well, except for the tanks.>

I wheeled. Scanned the line of flatcars. Nothing unusual. Nothing that wasn't supposed to be there.

Still, something prickled at the back of my brain. Something didn't seem right.

Battling aliens every day of my life has fine-tuned my already rampant paranoia.

I powered my wings and caught up to Tobias and the locomotive. A beautiful thermal radiated up the side of the mountain. I fanned my wing and tail feathers and soared on the billowing jet of warm air.

The freight train clattered below. One engine pulling a line of flatbed cars, loaded with military tanks. M-1 Abrams.

Yeah, M-1 Abrams. I knew them as well as I knew my own PlayStation. All those hours playing Tank Commando had finally paid off.

The M-1s belonged to the National Guard. They were chained one to a flatcar, their big guns rotated toward the back. And they were headed toward the city.

Truck and Humvee convoys had been snaking into town for days. Battalions of National Guard soldiers from all over the state were bunkered in Guard centers around the city.

Now they were bringing in tanks.

Ax had been monitoring all the local TV channels and the cable news networks, but nobody had mentioned a wide-scale urban training exercise. I couldn't find anything on the Internet, and the Chee hadn't heard anything from their Yeerk sources, either.

Tobias and I were here to do a little firsthand investigation. To find out if our state government had finally realized Earth was being invaded. To see if they were mounting a defense.

Or to see if this was a carefully laid out Yeerk plan. Were all those National Guard troops Controllers? Some of them, yeah. But all of them? We were talking thousands of soldiers. If they were all Controllers, we were in big trouble. We were talking serious doo-doo.

But we were betting they weren't. Hoping they weren't. Careful prior planning wasn't Visser One's usual MO. He usually jumped in with both feet and a lot of noise. And if the details didn't work themselves out, he just ripped a sub-visser's head off and plowed ahead with his next maniacal plan.

Besides, with a Blade ship and a fleet of Bug fighters at his disposal, the visser didn't need a bunch of clunky tanks.

On the other hand, Visser One had been pushing for all-out war. To wage war, you need an army. And if you need an army in a hurry, why not hijack an existing one? If the highest-ranking National Guard officers were Controllers, Visser One could easily round up the rest of the troops for a mass infestation of host bodies. And if he got the tanks out of the way, noninfested troops couldn't use them against him.

Chuk-chuk-chuk-chuk.

The freight train rolled along the tracks. It wasn't going all that fast for a train. About ten miles an hour. Maybe fifteen downhill.

But it was plenty fast for sustained, level, raptor flight. Tobias and I had started out over the engine, slipped back to the first flatcar, then the second. Now we were somewhere near the middle and losing ground. My wing muscles ached, burned, and finally went numb.

I wheeled again. Studied the train. Something still seemed odd. What was I missing?

Nothing, Marco. There's nothing scary on this

train. If there were, your raptor eyes would've seen it a mile off. You're just a paranoid freak.

A paranoid freak whose wings felt like they were going to snap off if I didn't stop flapping them.

<This is stupid,> I said. <We want to know where the tanks are going, right? The train's not going that fast. Why don't we just land on one and find out?>

I dove toward a flatcar in the middle of the train and swept over the top of the tank. My talons skidded across the big brass padlock on one of the top hatches. I locked them around a metal cargo cage, pulled my wings down, and hunkered against the bottom of the cage. Wind whipped the feathers on the top of my head.

A shadow slid over me. Tobias latched onto the hull of the tank, behind a big metal ring.

He hugged the metal. <Okay, this doesn't look too weird,> he said.

The train groaned down a steep hill. I turned my head. The column of tanks stretched out behind me, chugging through pine trees that towered above us on either side of the track. Sunlight filtered through the pine needles and flickered over the camouflage green of the tanks.

I saw no other movement. No life-forms, extraterrestrial or domestic.

Normal. Everything looked —

Wait. <No guards. If this is a National Guard operation gearing up to fight aliens, wouldn't they have soldiers posted on the train? And if it's Visser One, you know he'd have Controllers crawling all over. Thirty-four tanks, and *nobody's* watching them.>

<Oh, I wouldn't say that,> said Tobias.

I turned my head.

Another red-tailed hawk swooped around a curve ahead. Behind it, in formation, flew a squadron of golden eagles and peregrine falcons.

We were definitely not alone.

CHAPTER 2

The red-tailed hawk shot toward the train. The eagles and falcons followed, banking and diving above the tracks.

<They obviously don't have much flight experience.> Tobias directed his private thought-speak to me. <They're upwind. Flying in formation. A flock of eagles and the falcons acting like fighter pilots, taking orders from a hawk. These are not ordinary birds out for an afternoon of joy-flying.>

The eagles and falcons swooped past the locomotive and perched on the first tank. The red-tailed hawk hung in the air and watched the train pass under it. They hadn't seen us.

Yet.

Tobias slipped down the hull of the tank and crept underneath, into the dark cavern between the tank's tracks. Where he could see without being seen.

But I was on top. On the turret. I couldn't move without catching the hawk's eye. I pressed myself against the floor of the cargo basket and watched. Waited. Hoped my gray-and-white feathers blended in with the camouflage paint of the tank.

Right. We're talking about hawk vision here. No such thing as camouflage.

The red-tailed hawk kited above the train. Examined each car, each tank, that passed below.

<So, who are they?> I peered through the wire cage. Twelve of them. Two of us. <Or should we be overly optimistic and hope it's James and his gang?>

James and his gang. A group of auxiliary Animorphs we'd recently recruited to help us fight the Yeerks. Disabled kids by day. Superheroes by night. Or something like that.

The Animorphs — originally just five human kids and one Andalite — are trying to stop the Yeerks. I'm one of the human kids. Marco. That's all I'm going to tell you about me. No last name. No address.

Not that it probably makes any difference

anymore. The Yeerks know who I am. Or know who I was, anyway.

Yeerks. I'm sure you know all about them by now. If not, here's the condensed version: slimy gray slugs that slither into your ear canal, flatten themselves out over the surface of your brain, and seize control of your body. Parasitic aliens who are conquering Earth, one human at a time.

My mother was a Controller, controlled by one of the most powerful Yeerks in the Yeerk Empire, the former Visser One. We rescued her, killed the Yeerk who'd slithered into her head, staged a fake death for my dad and me, and evacuated to the mountain valley of the free Hork-Bajir.

Which should've been great. And it was. For me personally. And for my family. Okay, so we were on a never-ending camping trip with seven-foot-tall bladed aliens who rarely, if ever, bathed. And no, I hadn't seen an indoor toilet in weeks.

But I wasn't complaining. I had my mom back. Had my family back. And, as an added bonus, algebra homework was now only a distant, quickly fading memory.

But for the Animorphs, and for the war we were fighting, my mother's escape was the beginning of a long, terrifying, downhill slide. And we were about to hit rock bottom. Hard.

A big part of the reason we were struggling

9

was that the Yeerks had had better weapons than us. Plus, they outnumbered us about three gazillion to six. But we had a couple of advantages that helped level the playing field.

One: We could morph. We could touch an animal, acquire its DNA, then become that animal. A dying Andalite war-prince gave us that ability, and with it we could infiltrate, spy, destroy, and kick Yeerk butt in ways no human ever could. Two: Since morphing is Andalite technology, the Yeerks believed we were all Andalites. The former Visser Three, commander of the Yeerk invasion of Earth, had turned the planet upside down looking for a rogue band of blue aliens.

But he didn't find us, because he never looked in places we might actually be. Cozy suburban houses on tree-lined, *Leave-It-To-Beaver* streets. Noisy school hallways between classes. The food court at the mall. Not your typical Andalite hangouts. Well, except maybe the food court. After this war is over, I fully expect Ax, our resident Andalite, to spend the rest of his life in human morph at Cinnabon.

After we rescued my mother, though, it didn't take Visser Three long to figure out the "Andalite bandits" just might be human. He was promoted to Visser One, and he poured most of his resources into finding us.

The other Animorphs were forced to rescue

their families and flee to the Hork-Bajir valley. Rachel with her mom and two sisters. Cassie with her parents. Tobias with his mother.

And Jake. Alone.

We tried to get Jake's family out. Even Tom, his brother, who'd been a Controller since the beginning of the invasion. But the Yeerks got there first. Turned his mom and dad into Controllers, too.

Turned Jake into someone none of us knew anymore.

Ax moved to the valley, too. It had become our new sort of base.

Bottom line: We were human kids, and the Yeerks knew it. And we'd thought that was the worst thing that could happen to us.

We were wrong.

We needed more help. More firepower. More Animorphs. So we recruited humans we knew we could trust. Humans the Yeerks had written off. Humans they wouldn't infest.

Disabled kids.

The Yeerks caught on to what we were doing, and in the the last battle we lost the morphing cube. The blue box that gave anybody who touched it the power to morph. Our one weapon, the weapon Visser One had never been able to overcome, had fallen into Yeerk hands. Yeah, we could still morph. But now the Yeerks could, too.

Things were very, very bad.

I looked into the sky. The red-tailed hawk circled. Examined the tanks below. Its eyes locked onto mine.

Birds do not have lips. Birds cannot smile. But I swear this one did.

CHAPTER 3

"TSEEEEEEEER!"

The red-tailed hawk rocketed from the sky, eyes gleaming in triumph.

Chuk-chuk-chuk-chuk.

The freight train was giving me a free ride right toward my enemy.

I flapped to the top of the cargo bin and found a foothold.

<Marco?>

Tobias inched onto the bed of the flatcar. Four blocks of wood were wedged against the tank's tracks, two in front, two in back, keeping it from rolling. Tobias stood beside one of the front blocks, in its shadow, out of the hawk's line of vision.

<You do know a bird of prey is shooting from the sky, aiming for you, right?> he said.

<Uh, yeah.> My thought-speak actually sounded confident, like I really knew what I was doing. <The hawk doesn't have much bird experience, remember?>

I spread my wings. Flared my feathers. Fanned my tail. It's what raptors do when they're threatened. Make their bodies as large and menacing as possible.

What raptors do not do is plan suicidal fake-out maneuvers. No, that was purely a human move. My wings weren't spread high and wide just to make me look tough, though I'm sure I was one intense-looking bird. My wings were actually covering a thick steel tube that jutted up behind me through the cargo basket.

A steel tube I was betting the hawk, in his rush to skewer my guts, hadn't noticed.

I glared at him. Dared him to hit me.

"TSEEEEEEEEEEER!"

I stood my ground. Held my perch. My tail feathers flicked up and down like a lever, adjusting my balance to the movement of the train.

Tobias watched from the shadows, wings tense, ready to blindside the hawk if I failed.

The hawk plummeted, his beak aimed at my exposed chest.

Six feet above me. Four. Two.

Now!

I dove. Sideways and down, toward the hull of the tank.

Thungk-crack.

The red-tail slammed into the steel pipe above me.

Thump.

And fell backward into the cargo basket. He lay on the bottom of the cage, unmoving, his neck twisted back and to the side.

<That was a little on the crazy side, don't you think?> Tobias lifted his wings. <Now let's get away from here before his buddies notice he hasn't come up for air.>

The train rattled around a curve. We swooped over the side. Stayed low. And came beak to beak with the pack of golden-eagle-Controllers.

Did I mention that a golden eagle is almost three times as big as an osprey? That it's got about three times as much attitude and, in my opinion, is wound just a little too tight?

And that's just your regular, run-of-the-sky golden eagle. Stir in a crazed Yeerk and a terri-fied human host, and we're talking one seriously demented bird.

I cut sharply to the right. Tobias was already ahead of me. We powered our wings and shot toward the front of the train, six golden eagles on our tails.

Chuk-chuk-chuk-chuk.

The clatter of flatcars nearly drowned out the sound of beating wings. We whipped past one car. Another. We were gaining on the train.

The eagles were bigger. Meaner. But not as quick. If we could outlast them, we could outdistance them. I flapped my wings. We rounded the curve.

<Uh-oh,> said Tobias.

Five falcons circled above us. They weren't as big as the golden eagles. Not even as big as me or Tobias. But a whole lot faster.

One of the falcons peeled off. Dove!

<Oh, man. Not this again. I am so tired of being dive-bombed by birds.>

But this wasn't just any bird. This was a peregrine falcon. Not a bullet with feathers. A missile. A missile shooting toward me at two hundred miles an hour.

Which gave me zero time to think up a suicidal fake-out maneuver.

We were absolutely, positively toast.

CHAPTER 4

The falcon dropped from the sky. Another peregrine zeroed in on Tobias.

I pumped my wings. Scanned the rail bed, searching for an opening. A hiding place. A shield.

Nothing.

A wall of trees on one side. A freight train on the other. A flock of psycho-eagles behind.

<Under the train!> I yelled.

I dove between two flatcars. Tobias followed.

Chuk-chuk-chuk-chuk.

Metal grated against metal. We dodged under axles. Between wheels. Around brake boxes. It was reckless and desperate and stupid. Thousands of pounds of steel zinging along the tracks,

17

a fraction of an inch from our wings, our legs, our heads. One wrong move, one slight miscalculation, and we'd be chicken nuggets.

But it was our only chance.

We shot between the rail bed and the floor of the flatcars above. Lost an eagle. And another. A bird with a seven-foot wing span has no business under a moving freight train.

But the falcons kept coming. From the front. From behind. Raking. Slashing. Pummeling.

<Did you ever see that old movie *The Birds*?> I screamed.

<Not funny, Marco!> Tobias screamed back.

I jetted out from beneath a car, two falcons on my tail. I shot up. Around the tank. In. Out! Lost one of the falcons. Spun around the big gun. Lost the other.

<AAAAAAAHHHHHH!>

Talons the size of meat hooks clamped around my back, pierced feathers, then flesh, as a golden eagle plucked me from mid-flight.

I thrashed. Tried to wrench free. My skin ripped beneath the eagle's viselike grip. Claw scraped bone.

The eagle beat its wings and rose above the train. I dangled from its talons like a helpless field mouse, twisting and writhing.

<Marco! Get your wings out of the way!>

A flash of brown.

I tucked in my wings.

Tobias swept under the eagle in a Red-Tail Spiral of Death. His talons slashed the eagle's feathered legs.

"KYEEEEEEER!"

The eagle screamed. Banked. Turned to face his attacker.

But he wasn't as quick as Tobias, and he was weighted down by an uncooperative osprey.

"TSEEEEEEEEEEEEER!"

Tobias slammed into his throat.

The eagle veered. Raked a talon at Tobias. My neck fell from its clutches.

I spun, my butt clenched in one eagle claw, my head and shoulders flopping in midair, while Tobias and the eagle threw down above me.

Tobias circled. In. Out. Over. Around.

The eagle whirled and dodged.

<Is there a barf bag on this flight?> I said stupidly.

Tobias ripped his talons across the eagle's back.

The eagle lashed out, both feet open.

I was free!

I fell. Just plummeted toward the freight train below. Toward solid steel and jutting periscope housings.

Fly. I had to fly! I focused. I pulled my wings up. Out.

Air filled my wings, like I'd opened a parachute. Somewhere above me an eagle screamed. I had to circle. Get back to Tobias and help him fight off the eagle. I swept over the train. Around a tank.

<Marco, look out!>

Smack.

It hit me from below. A falcon that came out of nowhere. I lurched backward, end over end.

Thunk.

And landed on the bed of the flatcar.

CHAPTER 5

I lay on my back, wings splayed across rough wooden planks, belly exposed. Wind whipped my feathers. The flatcar swayed beneath me.

The falcon circled above. Flapped its wings and climbed. Gained altitude for another hit.

I closed my eyes. Shut out the clacking of the train, the screams of hawk and eagle. Ignored the crippling pain shooting through my body. Forced one image into my head: Marco. Healthy human Marco.

I felt my feathers liquefy. Felt them melt and dissolve into my skin. My legs thickened. Shot out to human length. The armored-plated scales covering them softened and smoothed into human skin.

But I was still bird from the legs up, and I still couldn't move. Pain burned through my wings. I refocused the image: arms.

Currrrrrrunnnnnnnch!

My wings straightened, stretched. The pain stretched, too. Longer. Thinner. Faded to a tingle, then disappeared as fingers popped from the ends of my arm-wings.

I flexed them. Opened my eyes.

I jerked to the side. Kicked at the falcon!

Talons skidded across my thigh and locked onto my flesh. The falcon squeezed a mass of muscle between its dagger-sharp toes and kept flying.

"AAAAAAAAAAAAAAHHHHHH!"

A golf ball-sized chunk of meat was ripped from my leg!

In human form, I could fend off the falcons.

In human form, I'd survive. Well, I'd survive longer than I would as an osprey.

But why volunteer for that kind of carnage?

I crawled to the tank. Sat with my back against the hull. Shoved the human image from my brain and thought of a different one: gorilla.

Want to bulk up? Forget bench presses and power shakes. Morph a gorilla.

I concentrated.

My chest and shoulders bulged. Stomach rippled. Biceps, deltoids, pecs. I was beefy. Buff.

My hands grew to the size of catchers' mitts. My fingers swelled to sausages.

Currrrreeeeeeeeek!

Human bones thickened. Arms shot out. My skull shifted. Back, then up. My face flattened. Jaw jutted forward. My skin darkened to a glistening black, and waves of coarse dark hair swept down my body.

I was Big Jim.

I leaped to the hull of the tank. The falcon dove and raked my arm. Another swept over my head, talons bared. A golden eagle swiped at my face.

But I was a gorilla. The eagle was merely an annoyance. A pest. As fierce as a mosquito but as easy to swat. I batted them away, like King Kong swatting airplanes from the top of the Empire State Building.

I turned and scanned the rail bed. The trees had thinned. The ground was leveling out. We were getting closer to the city.

Closer to Yeerk reinforcements.

Tobias shot around a tank three cars back, a golden eagle breathing down his neck. Two falcons buzzed and jabbed around him, taking whatever shots they could get.

<Tobias!> I yelled. <Time to bail.>

<You think?>

He flapped. Banked. Dove beneath the train.

The rail bed had been cut into the side of the hill. On one side the ground lay even with the bed of the flatcar.

Even with the tank's treads.

Four chains, as big around as my arm, ran from huge steel loops welded to the tank to more huge loops welded to the flatcar, two in front, two in back. Each pair of chains criss-crossed and were locked down tight by giant steel buckles in the middle of each chain.

Tools. I needed tools. Easy. I'd been to Level 10 in Tank Commando. I knew where to get them.

I leaped to the tank's hull. A big lockbox was built into the fender, the lid bolted shut with a brass padlock.

Simply not a problem for a gorilla. I ripped the lock loose, the brass folding in my fist like Play-Doh. Banged open the lid.

Yes! Ax. Shovel. Mondo-huge wrench. Pointy chisel-looking bar.

Sledgehammer.

I pulled the sledgehammer from the box. Leaped to the back of the tank.

The wood blocks were still wedged against the tank's treads, anchored by steel spikes driven through the blocks into the bed of the flatcar.

WHAM!

One block was airborne.

WHAM!

The other flew into the trees.

I grabbed one of the big metal buckles and gave it a twist. The chain loosened. I twisted both buckles till I had plenty of slack, then leaped onto the tank and unhooked the chains from the steel loops.

CLANG!

The chains slid to the floor of the flatcar.

The big gun was locked down into a bracket on the rear of the tank's hull. Since I was back there anyway, I ripped it free and leaped to the front of the tank.

WHAM! WHAM!

Wood blocks flew.

I twisted. Leaped. Unhooked. The front chains fell away.

The tank was free.

<Tobias! Let's go.>

I leaped onto the turret. Knuckle-walked to one of the hatches leading inside. Twisted the padlock off and hurled it at the eagle on Tobias's tail. Ripped the hatch open. Tobias shot through, into the tank.

I swatted the eagle away, then heaved the sledgehammer at the train's engine. It sailed end over end, over the flatcars.

Slammed onto the roof of the locomotive and bounced.

EEEEEEEEEE!

Brakes squealed. The flatcar lurched.

I barreled into the tank and slammed the lid.

Bye-bye birdies.

CHAPTER 6

<Okay. Good.> I squinted in the semidarkness. The train had stopped. <We're safe.>

<Uh-huh.> Tobias flapped up onto a metal box. <Sealed inside a tin can, with Yeerk-infested birds nesting on top, waiting for reinforcements who will peel the lid off and kill us. We're not safe, Marco. We're dead.>

<Dead? I think not. You underestimate the power of this particular tin can.> I patted the mesh wall behind me.

The inside of the turret was a round metal basket. Everything in it — walls, floor, storage bins, equipment — had been painted white. Seats and storage bins filled the front and mid-

27

dle. My knees banged against a big metal box. An ammo rack jabbed my shoulder.

The tank just wasn't built for a gorilla.

I demorphed and climbed into one of the seats. I peered through the vision block mounted above me. It was the gunner's site. Computerized. Equipped with night vision and infrared sensors. Just like the video game.

I could see the eagles and falcons. They were perched on the hull of the tank, waiting. The railroad guys were hiking along the tracks, searching the cars, searching under the cars, searching the trees. One of them was carrying the sledgehammer. Both of them looked really confused and a little ticked off.

I climbed from my seat. Stood in the center of the basket and tried to figure out what to do first.

"I assume we'll be taking this buggy for a joyride." Tobias had morphed into his human self. "If we can figure out how to start it."

"What do you mean, *if* we can figure out how to start it? You happen to be sitting next to the Tank Commando master of the Hork-Bajir valley."

"Right. Video-game expertise." He glanced around at the switches and levers. "So, what, we just rev it up and barrel off the side of the train?"

"Yeah. The train's stopped. The ground's almost level with the flatcar. Should be easy. I saw a tank crew do it on the History Channel."

"Ah. Video games and cable. How reassuring." He pulled a helmet from a hook on the side of the turret. "I should probably wear this."

"Probably. That piece in front is a microphone," I said. "And the ear thingies are speakers."

The mike was attached to a thick wire that curved down from the side of the helmet, like a telephone headset. Tobias adjusted it in front of his mouth.

"I feel like Britney Spears," he said.

"Unfortunately for me, you don't look like her. Sit here. Plug the cord in and push that little switch forward so you can talk to me."

I climbed through the crawl space between the turret and the driver's area. Everything down there was painted white, too. I slid into the seat. It tipped back so far I was almost lying down. I slipped my helmet on. Plugged it in.

And took a deep breath.

I'll let you in on a little secret. Gunning down enemy troops in a video game does not actually prepare you to operate a real-life, sixty-ton tank. I mean, yeah, the controls looked familiar. I gripped the handlebar in front of me. And the equipment was all in basically the same spots as it was on my PlayStation screen.

But this was the real deal. If I flipped the tank over, I couldn't hit ESCAPE and start again.

29

"How's it going down there?" Tobias's voice crackled into my helmet.

"Cool." I studied the instrument panel. "Everything's cool. Got it all figured out."

Which, I realized, was almost true. Because here's another little secret: Tank controls are amazingly well-marked. FUEL. START. MASTER SWITCH. It didn't take a genius to figure out how to get it rolling.

Was the army aware of this? Did they realize that, with a little trial and error, a third grader with a limited vocabulary could probably steal an entire tank?

I settled back into my seat. Pushed MASTER SWITCH. Heard a little hum as the instrument panel lit up.

I peered through my vision block. It wasn't a whiz-bang computerized periscope like the gunner's sight. It was more like a window. A slit of a window fitted with thick, bulletproof glass. The eagles and falcons were still perched on the tank. And they obviously knew something was up. They fluttered their feathers and stared at each other.

I pushed START.

RrrrrRRRRRRrrrrrrrmmmmmm.

The engine spun up and fired. Out on the hull, our friends the birds screeched and flapped their wings.

Okay. I could do this. I gripped the handlebar thing. Right grip, throttle. Left grip, transmission. Gear switch under my left thumb.

I took a breath. In about a minute we'd either be off the flatcar, ripping over the hills, or we'd be flipped over on the rail bed, like a big old metal bug on its back.

I kept the transmission in neutral and turned the handlebar a sharp left, it was sort of like riding my bike. Sort of. Revved the throttle. The tank rotated sideways on the bed of the flatcar. Its treads hung out over the edge, facing the cutout section of hill.

I straightened the handlebar. Shifted to drive. Pulled back on the throttle.

And we lunged forward into empty space.

31

CHAPTER 7

The front of the treads rolled over the edge of the flatcar, supported by nothing. I could see level ground ahead. I held the throttle steady.

The tank tipped, nose down. The falcons and eagles bailed. They obviously had no confidence in my tank-driving abilities.

"Uh, Marco?" Neither, apparently, did Tobias.

WHOOOOOOMPH!

The tracks hit solid ground.

The tank hung halfway on the flatcar, half on the cutout part of the hill.

Then the treads grabbed onto the dirt and pulled us from the flatcar. We crawled across the cleared area next to the tracks. I found an opening in the line of trees, and we rattled off through the woods.

"Cake," I said.

I was very impressed with the tank. And, of course, myself. The M-1 clipped right along. It was a tank, but it could move. Anywhere. Up hills, over boulders, across ditches.

I bounced along in the driver's seat. Bushes crumbled and disappeared under my treads. Okay, and a couple of trees, too. And the corner of a railroad storage shed. It took me a while to get used to the steering.

The bird-Controllers had settled back onto the tank, their talons locked around hinges and handles, their wings bowed down against the hull.

My helmet crackled. "Call me crazy," said Tobias, "but when we abort a mission, I don't think we should bring the Yeerks home with us."

I heard a rattle above and behind me. The tank's big gun whipped to the front of the tank. Knocked a golden eagle out cold. He fell from the tank. The gun swung to the rear and then around to the front again. The other birds took to the skies.

"Tobias? That was you, wasn't it?"

"Yeah. I found an operating manual back here. Pretty dry reading, but there's some stuff in it we can definitely use."

We thundered across a clearing. Slogged through a stream. Climbed the steep bank on the other side like it was downhill. Rattled through the underbrush and back into the trees. The bird-Controllers swooped overhead.

Tobias spun the gun again. The eagles and falcons screeched and flapped toward the sky.

I thundered along, the turret basket whirling inches behind my head, trying not to get the gun tube stuck in the side of a hill or caught in a tree.

Trying to keep my eyes focused through the vision block. The woods flashed by in a blur.

THUNNNNNG.

The tank tipped sideways. Kept rolling. Thumped back to level ground.

"This is way cooler than a tank sim," said Tobias. "Think Jake'd let us keep an M-1 up in the . . . Marco! Watch out!!"

"Watch what? I can't see very well."

"I know. But I can. Stop. Stop!"

I pushed down on the brake. The tank jerked to a stop. I bounced forward, then back. I peered through my vision block.

And all I saw was sky. Acres and acres of empty air. We'd left the woods and were perched on the edge of a cliff overlooking the Interstate.

The falcons and eagles had disappeared. Smart birds.

My helmet sputtered. "Uh, Marco? Does this thing have reverse?"

I glanced at the gear switch. "Yeah."

I pressed the switch with my thumb. Gave it gas. The tank started to roll. Forward.

"AAAAAAAAAAAAHHHHHHHHHHH!" Tobias screamed in my ear.

I slammed on the brake. The tank stopped. Chunks of earth crumbled beneath the treads and plummeted from the cliff.

"Not reverse," I said.

"No kidding."

I pressed the gear switch again. Twisted the throttle toward me a fraction of a centimeter.

The tank inched backward.

I cranked the throttle. Backed to the edge of the woods. Sat in the shadow of the trees and let the tank idle.

The "cliff" was a hill the highway department had blasted through when they built the Interstate. It sloped down on either side till it was level with the road.

I cranked the handlebar. Turned the tank. We thundered down the hill. I turned again. Plowed through the ditch and up onto the highway.

"Uh, Marco? You sure you know what you're doing?" Tobias said.

"Sure. This puppy can do sixty-five, no sweat."

"Yeah, sixty-five in the wrong direction!"

I stared out at the highway. It was divided, with a concrete barrier between the two sides. And our side was going the wrong way.

Not much I could do about that but keep going. And hope the other vehicles were smart enough to get out of the way.

They were.

A brand-new Lexus shrieked off to the side of the road. A rusty old pickup filled with wood planks followed it.

A minivan driven by a soccer-mom skidded after them. An SUV driven by a guy in a suit swerved right behind.

So far, everyone was working with us.

Except for the eighteen-wheeler.

It kept on barreling toward us. I slowed down. Veered toward the shoulder. Plowed over a bank of road signs. Veered back onto the highway to avoid a stalled-out jeep.

Still the truck bore down on us. We were close enough now so I could see the driver's face. He was smiling. No, he was laughing.

"Is the guy a total idiot?" Tobias cried. "He's playing chicken with a tank. A tank!"

"He is bigger."

"Yeah? Well, we're better equipped."

The big gun rattled. Swung to the right.

"You can't shoot him, Tobias!"

"He doesn't know that."

The cannon rattled again. Up, this time. Straight at the truck's window.

The trucker's smile froze. He cranked his steering wheel and swerved into the next lane.

"That'll learn him," I muttered.

CHAPTER 8

Jake frowned. "So, where did you leave the tank?"

Tobias and I looked at each other.

We were back in the Hork-Bajir valley, seated around the campfire outside my parents' cabin. Crickets hummed. The setting sun bathed the valley in amber rays. Champ, Tobias's mom's dog, drowsed at our feet. It was peaceful. It was nice.

It was a council of war.

The Joint Chiefs of Staff were all present. Me, Tobias, Rachel, Cassie, Jake, and Ax. And, since we'd moved to the valley, we'd added two more members.

Toby, the Hork-Bajir seer. Seer, meaning

smarter than the average Hork-Bajir. Meaning two-plus-two actually held some meaning for her. So did quantum physics.

The second new member was my mom.

"The tank." I took a breath. "Well, you know Chapman's house? Nice two-story?"

Jake sighed. "How many stories is it now?"

"Uh . . ." I glanced at Tobias. "Zero? But the back deck will give Chapman a nice supply of firewood this winter. It's already piled up for him."

Tobias smiled. "Too bad he doesn't have a fireplace anymore."

"Excuse me?" said Rachel. "You flattened Melissa's house?"

She stared at me. She and Melissa Chapman used to be friends. Back before Melissa's dad became a Controller and Rachel became an Animorph.

She turned on Tobias. "And you went along with it?"

"Whoa. Down, girl," I said. "You're just mad because you didn't get to drive a tank. Nobody got hurt. Nobody was home. Not even Fluffer McNutter or whatever that stupid cat's name is."

"Fluffer McKitty," she said.

"Oh. Excuse me. Fluffer McKitty. That's so much better. Anyway, they're all fine. Melissa, her parents, her cat."

Tobias nodded. "They're just, well, homeless."

Rachel shook her head. Looked to Jake to back her up.

Jake said . . . nothing.

We waited for his reprimand. For his poorly concealed amusement. For his: "That's not exactly what I meant by low profile, Marco." All the normal Jake stuff.

The fire popped. Somebody's nylon jacket squeaked. Ax nailed a mosquito with the flat of his tailblade.

Jake sighed again and poked the campfire with a stick.

I frowned. Looked at Ax. He shrugged, one of the many human gestures he'd picked up.

Since we'd moved to the valley, Jake had been on autopilot. I didn't know how to talk to him anymore. This was Jake. My best friend since second grade, and I couldn't even have a superficial, meaningless conversation with him.

Let alone try to get into his head.

Part of it was me. My guilt. Yeah, big news flash, call the Associated Press, Marco feels guilty. Well, wouldn't you? My family was safe, recovered, together, while Jake's had been torn away from him. There was only a very slim chance he'd ever get them back.

But that wasn't exactly why I felt guilty.

I felt guilty because I was so happy. Happy

my mom was back. Happy that she and my dad were still nauseatingly in love. My best friend had lost everything that had ever meant anything to him. Meanwhile, I practically had to tie myself to a tree to keep from running up and down the valley, arms spread wide, belting out show tunes.

I glanced at Cassie. She sat on top of the old picnic table Ax and I had found and dragged to the camp. She sat away from the fire. Away from the whole group.

I figured if anybody could get through to Jake, Cassie could. I mean, she's Cassie, for pete's sake. But since our last mission, since the Yeerks had stolen the morphing cube, Jake was more distant from her than from anybody. Distant? Actually where Cassie was concerned, Jake had completely closed down. Like an iron door had slammed shut.

"But did you get any information?" Toby looked at Tobias, then me. She was crouched in the grass, the light from the smoldering logs intensifying the fire in her Hork-Bajir eyes. "Did you discover anything useful?"

Tobias scratched Champ's ears. "You mean before we stole government property, endangered innocent motorists, and leveled a moderately priced suburban home?"

"Yes." She nodded.

"Well, we did manage to get a good look at

41

the train," I said. "The National Guard wasn't moving those tanks. Not the regular, uninfested National Guard anyway."

"The uninfested National Guard." Jake nodded. Stirred the fire. "We've been assuming there still is such a thing." He turned to my mom. "Eva, is there any chance we're wrong?"

"No." Mom shook her head. "If Visser Three had taken over the National Guard while I was Visser One's host body, I'd have known about it. What am I saying? Everybody would've known about it. Visser Three would've made sure."

"What about since then?" said Jake. "Since he was promoted to Visser One?"

"No." Mom shook her head again. "Not enough time. We're talking thousands of soldiers, spread out over the entire state. And they're not on active duty. They're weekend warriors, so most of the time they're not even with their units. This is a huge operation. It'd take months to plan, months more to execute."

"Okay." Jake paced. Poked his stick at the fire. "With all the troop movement over the last few days, we can assume the planning stage is done. So I'm assuming the execution stage is beginning. We can also assume at least some of the highest ranking officers are Controllers. Otherwise, the visser wouldn't be able to get all those soldiers into the city. They'll all be infested. Soon. We can't let that happen."

<But how can we be sure we can stop it?> Ax asked. His blue fur gleamed in the firelight. <Even with James and the other new Animorphs, are we big enough?>

"No. We're not. We need help." Pace. Pace. Poke. "So, we split up. One group is the in-your-face group." Jake glanced at Rachel. "That group creates a diversion with the National Guard troops. Keeps them away from the Yeerk pool as long as possible. They're stationed all over the city, so we'll have to keep moving to hit all the bases. But it'll also split Visser One's resources, trying to stop us. It'll keep him busy. Buy us some time."

"We have been planning to liberate the group of Hork-Bajir that guard The Sharing headquarters," said Toby. "We can be ready to go in the morning."

"Good. That'll be one more fire Visser One has to put out. Group Two will be smaller, quieter. They'll need to show a little more finesse."

"Finesse?" Rachel shot me a sideways look. "Oh, yeah. Some of us are *so* good at that."

"We'll have to be," said Jake. "Because only one person has enough authority to stop the movement of National Guard troops. The gover-

43

nor. Group Two has to travel to the capitol. Get to the governor somehow. Convince him to work with us."

"I'll go," Cassie said.

"No," Jake replied, practically before the words were out of her mouth.

Cassie froze. Stared at him.

Jake didn't even look at her.

Instead, he gave me a sarcastic half-smile. A glimpse of the old Jake. "If anybody can handle a politician, it's Marco. And Tobias can get to the capitol without getting lost. We also need to make sure the governor isn't a Controller, and Ax is the most qualified to judge. So that's the second group. Marco, Ax, and Tobias."

That's when he finally looked at Cassie. Locked his gaze on her.

"I can trust them," he said.

Silence.

Jake turned back to us and continued, "I'll be with Group One. Rachel. Cassie. Toby and some of her people. James's group, too. We'll try to stir up some major chaos before midnight. Marco, you need to reach the governor some time tomorrow. Doesn't matter exactly when, just get there."

He stopped pacing. Stopped poking the fire. Looked at me. At Ax and Tobias. "I know this sounds melodramatic, but we can't fight this war alone anymore. We need the authorities on our side. If the governor is free, you *have* to find a way to convince him. If he's a Controller, well, we'll have to figure out Plan B."

"Oh. Well," I said. "As long as there's no pressure."

"And try to keep things down. We don't need Visser One figuring out what we're up to." The half-smile again. "I'm counting on you guys to be cool. And to handle this the best way you know how."

"Be cool? Handle this? Marco?" Rachel shook her head. "We are in serious trouble."

CHAPTER 9

Weeds slapped at our faces. Mud sucked at our feet — well, two of us anyway. We waded into the swamp and crouched behind a stand of cattails. Me, Ax, Tobias perched on Ax's shoulder. Group Two. The ones with "finesse."

We were at The Gardens, in the wetlands section that divided the zoo from the amusement park. The sun was rising behind the Ferris wheel. An early morning fog rose from the water.

Birds filled the big, marshy pond. Ducks, geese, swans, pelicans, cranes. Flamingoes.

<Hey,> said Tobias. <We can morph lawn ornaments.>

The capitol was over two hundred miles away. The fastest way to get there was by air, and our normal bird-of-prey morphs wouldn't do the job. We needed distance flyers. Ducks. Our plan was to get in, acquire the necessary DNA, and get out before The Gardens opened for the day.

And at the edge of the water, near our cattail hideout, swam a family of mallards.

We hunkered down and waited for them to drift closer.

"Anybody know the best way to catch a duck?" I whispered.

Ax peered through the cattails. <I have been observing these animals very closely.> His main eyes studied a group of ducklings, while his stalk eyes followed a big male duck that bobbed near the cattails. <They are quick and agile, but they spend a great deal of time with their heads underwater.>

<They're eating,> Tobias explained.

<Ah.> Ax nodded. <You see how much safer and more efficient it would be for them if they fed through their feet? Capturing a member of this species while its front half is submerged should be relatively simple.>

Simple. Right. When was the last time anything in our lives was simple?

The male paddled into the cattails. I could tell he was a male, a drake, by his shimmery green head, his cinnamon-brown chest, and the band of white that divided the two like a necklace. In the duck world, the boys get to be the pretty ones. All the girl ducks were a drab, splotchy brown.

The drake swam closer. Dipped his beak into the water.

I raised my arms. Slowly. I tensed, ready to grab him as soon as he dove for food.

Sploot.

Something heavy and wet landed on my head. Part of it slid down my face and latched on to my cheek.

"Gree-deep," said the heavy, wet thing.

Great. I lifted my hand. Started to shove it off. The drake drifted closer. I froze.

<Marco, do you realize that there is a large amphibian on your head?>

<It's a bullfrog, Ax-man,> said Tobias.

"Gree-deep," said the frog.

The mallard turned. Watched me. Paddled away.

I poked the bullfrog.

"Oh, man." I groaned. "I think it just peed on me."

I started to poke him again, then stood very still. One of the female mallards had paddled into the cattails.

She nipped at something in the water. Floated. Nipped again. Plunged her head beneath the surface. Her bottom bobbed on top.

I lunged. Grapped the duck around the middle. Held her wings tight to her body and pulled her from the water.

She thrashed and quacked. The other ducks squawked and flapped away.

I turned toward shore. The frog slid down my face and over my eyes.

I flung my head, tried to shake him loose. Kept my grip on the duck. Reeled blindly in the water.

"QUAAAAAAAAAAACK."

The duck let out a cry and wrenched a wing from under my grip. Beat it against my arm, my face. Lashed out with her feet.

You think just because they're webbed, duck feet don't have claws? They do. And they're sharp. Two kicks shredded my forearms.

"AAAAAAAAHHHHHH!"

I screamed. The pond erupted in quacks, honks, and screeches. Water sprayed over me. Cattails sliced at my face.

The bullfrog stayed planted on my head.

I stood totally still and concentrated on the duck in my hands. On the duck that was kicking, flapping, flailing. I had to focus. Had to acquire it before it got away.

"QUAAAAAAAAAAACK."

Something small, hard, and sharp clamped down on my nose.

"AAAAAAAAAAAAAHHHHHHHHHH!"

I screamed. The duck had bit me! She gave one more major thrash and slipped from my hands.

"QUAAAAAAAAAACK."

Her wings beat against my face as she flapped away.

"Gree-deep."

The frog leaped into the cattails.

"Oh, now you decide to leave," I said. I slogged toward the bank.

<Stay still, Marco. I believe I have one.> Ax vaulted into the pond in a beautiful, perfect arc, his Andalite form clearly outlined in the morning sun.

"Daddy, Daddy! Look! It's a unicorn."

I whirled.

A little girl was pulling her dad toward the duck pond. A group of grade-school kids on a field trip jostled along the sidewalk behind them.

"The park's open," I yelled to Ax and Tobias. "Let's get what we came for and get out!"

"A blue unicorn, Daddy. Look!"

"There's no such thing as a unicorn, sweetheart. That's a, well, it's a . . . an antelope. Yes, an antelope. That's it. Probably from . . . Africa. An African antelope."

Ax, the blue Andalite/African antelope, splashed through the water, chasing the mallard.

50

Ducks and geese quacked, honked, and thrashed over the pond. I sloshed after him, into the path of oncoming birds, trying to nab one as it flapped by. I could hear the field trip kids shouting behind me.

"Hey, what's that kid doing in the water?"

"Looks like he's target practice for those birds."

"Can we go swimming, too, Mrs. Duncan, please?"

I dove. Ax lunged. Ducks skidded across the water.

<I'll handle this,> Tobias said.

He took to the sky and circled. Spilled air from his wings and dove. Swooped over the water and landed easily on a mallard's back. The duck squawked and splashed and tried to fly away. Tobias sank his talons into its feathers. The duck relaxed. It had fallen into an acquiring trance.

<Marco. Your turn,> said Tobias.

I splashed out to the duck. Grabbed him around the middle. Pressed my hands against his feathers. Had to start acquiring him before he snapped out of it.

I shut out the squawks and squeals around me, the shouts and laughs from the shore. Concentrated on the duck.

"Ax. You ready?" I sloshed toward him, duck in hand.

51

Ax reached for it.

"Andalite!"

I spun. One of teachers pushed her way through the mob of field trip kids. She knocked a zoo guard onto the concrete and pulled a gun from his holster.

CHAPTER 10

"Ax! Get back!"

Ax dove into the cattails.

I dove after him, still carrying the droopy duck.

Woooooooooosh.

What I guess was a tranquilizer dart pierced the weeds.

I handed the duck off to Ax in a weird DNA water relay.

TSSSSSEEEEEEEEEW-buh-loooooosh.

A Dracon beam vaporized the water beside me. Human-Controllers leaped into the pond and splashed toward the cattails.

Others, still on the bank, began changing. Shrinking, shifting . . . morphing. A leopard

53

emerged from a security guard, a golden eagle from an ice-cream vendor.

<Man, I liked it better when only we could do that,> I said.

<I've got the eagle,> Tobias called from overhead.

"TSEEEEEEEEEEEEEER!"

He dove. Hit the eagle before it had finished the morph. Circled for another shot.

"RoaaAAAAAAAAWWWWWWWWWWR."

The leopard leaped at Ax, teeth bared.

Fwap! Fwap!

Ax, still holding the duck, struck back with his bladed tail.

TSSSSSEEEEEEEEW-buh-loooooosh.

Human-Controllers charged through the pond, firing Dracons.

I took a deep breath. Filled my lungs with air and dove into the shallow water.

I focused. Tried not to move. Tried not to make waves or bubbles.

And then it started. I felt my muscles bulge. Bones realign. Felt pin prickles as fur popped from my skin.

But I was running out of air! My lungs burned. My eyes burned. Still, I concentrated. Felt my skull bulge. My jaw jut forward.

Finally, I erupted from the water. Gulped in air. Tore through the cattails and leaped onto the bank. I was Marco the gorilla. And I was looking to kick some Controller butt.

TSSSSSSSEEEEEEEEW!

A Dracon beam fried the cattails. I whirled. A human-Controller stood at the edge of the water. He raised his handheld Dracon and aimed it at my chest.

I leaped. Knocked the Dracon into the water with one fist. Slammed the Controller unconscious with the other.

More human-Controllers charged me from behind. Jumped onto my back. Beat me with sticks and rocks and cell phones. One of the Controllers jabbed at my eyes with her car keys.

I whirled. Flung the Controllers away, one by one. One by one they sailed over the sidewalk and —

CRASH!

— flattened a slush stand.

"HONNNK. HONNNK."

A goose flapped up from the pond. It flew low, straight at me.

Another Controller? I lifted an arm, ready to swing. Ready to fend off its claws and beak.

But the goose just continued to beat its wings. It flew over my head toward the zoo. Not a Controller. Just a goose.

This was insane. Birds were starting to make me jumpy.

The battle had spilled into the amusement park section of The Gardens. Tobias and the eagle were locked in aerial combat above the roller coaster.

Ax galloped toward the merry-go-round. The leopard lay beside it, trying to drag itself underneath on three legs.

Ax stood above the leopard, tail blade poised.

"RoaaAAAAAAAAWWWWWWWWWR."

<Ax! Watch out!>

A cougar vaulted from the top of the merry-go-round. Sunk teeth and claws into Ax's back.

Fwap! Fwap-fwap!

Ax's tail blade lashed out.

Wooooosh.

Another tranquilizer dart shot past my head. Rippled the fur on my shoulder. I wheeled. Two human-Controllers stood at the edge of the log ride, on top of the waterfall. One held a gun.

TSSSSSEEEEEEEEEWWW!

The other wielded a Dracon.

I knuckle-leaped toward the log ride.

TSSSSSEEEEEEEEEWWW!

The concrete beneath me exploded.

I bounded over the wooden fence that separated the log ride from the sidewalk. Climbed through the synthetic jungle up the man-made mountain.

I was a gorilla. This was my territory. Okay, so

the jungle was fiberglass and plastic, whatever. I tore through it anyway. Reached the top of the waterfall in fifteen seconds flat. The Controllers stood on the edge of the man-made river, peering out over the park. I ripped through a tangle of fake vines and leaped onto the edge of the riverway.

"AAAAAAAAAAAAAAAAAAH!"

They screamed. I hammered.

BAM! BAM!

Spuh-LOOOOOOOSH!

They plunged into the river.

"AAAAAAAAAAAAAAaaaaaaaahhhhhh . . ."

And shot over the waterfall.

"KYEEEEEER!"

A golden eagle's scream. I was above the roller coaster, and I could see down over the track, where an eagle and Tobias were still at it. The eagle screamed again and pummeled Tobias.

Tobias fell, one wing flapping, the other hanging limp at his side.

He spiraled. Down. Down.

<Tobias!>

Thump.

And landed on the elevated track of the roller coaster, in a dip at the bottom of a steep hill.

A roller-coaster car filled with passengers clanked up the other side of the hill.

57

<Get up! Tobias, get up!>

I bounded along the edge of the fiberglass river.

The eagle hurtled toward Tobias, ready to finish him off.

The roller-coaster car reached the top of the hill and shot down the other side. It picked up speed as it traveled. Passengers squealed and flung their arms above their heads.

Tobias fluttered his good wing. His body flopped pitifully against the steel track.

He was too weak to get out of the way. It was too late!

<Tobias! No!>

CHAPTER 11

"KYEEEEEEEEER!"

The eagle plummeted.

The roller-coaster car shot down the tracks. Hurtled toward the badly injured body of my friend.

<Tobias!> I skidded down the side of the waterfall, from tree to vine to bush.

The eagle was directly above him now.

The roller-coaster car almost on top of him.

Wuuuumpf.

<What the . . . !>

The roller-coaster car slammed into the eagle! Brown and golden feathers spewed over the passengers.

"AAAAAAAAAAAAAAHHHHHHHH!"

59

Women screamed. Kids cried. Men shouted.

But I wasn't interested in the passengers.

More brown feathers flashed below. Then, a red tail. A hawk had dropped through the bottom of the elevated tracks.

<Tobias?>

He flapped and swooped toward the sky, both wings strong and healthy.

<What happened?!> I asked.

<No big deal.> He climbed above the tracks. <I just stole your suicidal fake-out maneuver, that's all.>

<That's all? Can a gorilla have a heart attack? Because I think I'm having a heart attack. I'm not breathing right. You know that was *completely* insane, don't you?>

<Insane, yes. But it worked.> He flapped over the waterfall. <Where's Ax?>

BANG! CLANK!

A tram car rocked and swayed overhead, on its way from the amusement park to the zoo.

WHAM.

The door banged open, and Ax leaped out, a cougar wrapped around its neck.

They dropped, a ball of cat and alien, free-falling to Earth.

Ax began shrinking. His blue fur melted into a shimmering swirl of green and chestnut feathers. His stalk eyes shriveled. His front legs dissolved.

His back hooves flattened and webbed out as his arms broadened into wings. He slipped from the cougar's grasp and flapped toward the sky.

<NOOOOOOOOOOOOOOOOO!>

The cougar's thought-speak echoed through the park. He writhed, twisted, tried to get all four feet beneath him. He dropped through the trees into the Siberian tiger exhibit.

"RrrrrrrrrrOOOOOOOOAAAAAAAAWWWWWW RRR!"

Big kitty battle cries erupted from the pen.

<That should keep him busy for a while,> said Tobias.

He and Ax landed beside me in the man-made jungle. Tobias went mallard. I demorphed then concentrated on the duck.

I'd morphed birds before. A seagull. And an osprey, of course. The osprey and mallard were roughly the same size. But they were built a whole lot different.

The ground shot up as my body shrank. I put out a hand to steady myself, but my fingers were already thinning, shifting. My first two fingers shot out. My pinkie and ring finger dissolved into nothing.

Splooooooooooot.

My bones snapped, realigned, and became hollow. Internal organs moved, re-formed. New ones sloshed into existence. My shoulders shifted up. My hips shifted back. My whole body tipped forward till I was lying on my face.

<Well, this is comfortable,> I said.

My mouth and nose melded together and jutted into the ground. My nostrils slid to the top, and my neck shot straight out, scraping my nose/mouth combo through the dirt. The combo flattened out. Hardened into a long, broad bill.

Sccccuuuurreeeeech.

Orange scales shot down my legs. Claws erupted from my toes, and the skin between them webbed together.

I was a duck. Short, squat, steady. Alert. Tense. A little skittish, maybe, but ready to stand my ground, to defend my territory. In your face, if I had to. And — this part is gross — suddenly overcome by a craving for mosquito larva.

<Ewwww.>

I shuddered and tried out my new mallard voice: "Kwek." It didn't sound right. Too low. Too raspy. I tried again. "Kwek. Kwek-kwek-kwek-kwek."

<I think we acquired a defective duck,> I said. <My quack's not coming out right.>

<I know a little something about birds,> said Tobias. <And when it comes to mallards quacking, the females are better at it.>

<Ah. So it's a trade-off. A pretty face.> I tilted

62

my shimmering green head. <Or a big, full-bodied quack.>

<The quack's not the big problem,> said Tobias. <What I'd really like to know is, who thought up this leg/tail arrangement?> He waddled between two fiberglass trees. <Look at my butt.>

<Uh, thanks, Tobias. I think I'll pass.>

<Seriously,> he said. <I'm sure it's great for swimming, having the motor in the rear like that, but walking? My legs are so far apart my whole back end bobs up and down every time I take a step. Up and down. Side to side. Like a . . . like a . . .>

<Like a duck?>

<Yeah. It's humiliating.> He swept a wing over his flat duck bill. <And this is just wrong.>

<Tobias, you've been a hawk way too long.> I lifted my wings. <Let's go find the governor.>

CHAPTER 12

I pushed off with my feet, flapped my wings, and sprung straight into the air. Through the trees. Above the waterfall.

<Hey, this is cool,> I said. <No long, running takeoffs. No flapping along the ground. When the duck wants to be in the air, he's in the air.>

Tobias and Ax followed, and we flew over The Gardens. Three identical ducks, morphed from the same DNA.

A flock of seagulls flitted about the food court. We watched them. Listened. Two of the birds suddenly took to the sky.

Controllers? We beat our wings and veered away, looking for a place to land. A place to defend ourselves. The gulls dove for a Frito bag lying behind a trash can. Not Controllers. Just hungry scavengers. We headed back on course.

<I don't believe I'm saying this.> Tobias. <But I can almost sympathize with Visser One. Now we know what he's been going through all this time. Dodging every animal he sees, thinking the boogeyman in morph is lurking around every corner.>

We decided three ducks flying by themselves looked a little conspicuous, especially to Controllers who were probably looking for three ducks flying by themselves. So we hooked up with a flock of mallards heading in the direction of the capitol.

We leeched onto the back of their V formation, and flapped off over the mountains.

This wasn't sleek, soaring raptor flight. With our round heads, long necks, and plump bodies, we looked more like bowling pins with wings.

I was the Energizer Bunny with feathers. The Energizer Birdie. I flapped and flapped and flapped. Fifty miles an hour on a straight, level flight.

<Here's a question,> I said. <Why haven't we morphed ducks before? All those times we had to fly long distances, like trying to keep up with the train yesterday, Tobias. Or that time Jake got his

65

guts squashed on the ceiling when we were stowing away in fly morph on an airplane. Why didn't anybody say, "Long distance? Let's go duck"?>

<Yes,> Ax agreed. <This is a useful morph. I'm not tired after quite a bit of time in the air.>

<Exactly. Plus we're flying in formation, and it looks normal. None of that bird-of-prey stuff where we have to fly miles apart and pretend we don't know each other. No offense, Tobias. I like swooping and gliding and riding the thermals as much as the next raptor, but every bird can't be a fighter jet. Sometimes you need a steady, reliable 747.>

I scanned the rocks and treetops below. The duck had decent eyesight. It didn't have binocular vision like an osprey, so I couldn't judge distances very well. I couldn't scope out a fish from half a mile away and know exactly when to dive and at what speed and where to plunge my talons into the water to catch it.

But hey, the mallard didn't need that kind of information. Mosquito larva and barley seed don't move very fast.

We left the mountains behind and flew over fields and rivers, highways and small towns. We took a mid-morning pitstop on a marshy farm pond, then the flock headed back to the sky. We flew high to take advantage of a nice tailwind and reached the outskirts of a city just before noon. A large white dome gleamed in the distance.

<This is it,> I said. <I recognize the capitol from our third-grade field trip.>

<A domed building?> Ax's thought-speak was filled with awe. He has a thing for domed roofs. <Excellent living quarters! Well-suited for an important government leader.>

<That's not where he lives, Ax-man. It's just where he works.>

<And it's Saturday,> said Tobias. <So chances are, he's not there.>

<So chances are, he'll be at home,> I said.

<Which is . . . ?>

I didn't say anything.

Ax let out a raspy quack. <We traveled all this way, and we do not know where we are going?>

<No big deal,> I said. <We've got finesse, remember? We'll ask directions.>

We discreetly peeled off from the flock and landed in a big mud puddle behind a truck stop. Ax and Tobias dabbled in the water. I waddled across the gravel to the men's room, waited until it was empty, and demorphed.

I circled to the front of the building and went inside. A skinny woman with teased orange hair sat behind the cash register, leafing through a magazine.

"Um, hi," I said. "I'm from out of town, doing a little sight-seeing, and I'm wondering how to get to the governor's mansion."

She didn't look up from the magazine. "Beats me. The governor's never invited me over."

She flipped to a page of makeup tips. I wandered through the side door to the truck stop's diner.

None of the waitresses knew where the governor lived. They hollered back to the kitchen, but the cook and the dishwasher were clueless, too.

"Thanks anyway," I said.

I headed toward the door.

"Need directions?"

I turned. Two bikers were eating lunch at the counter. The big one was looking at me. He bit off a mouthful of burrito and watched me as he chewed.

Did I say he was the big one? I take that back. He wasn't big. He was huge. His left bicep was bigger than my whole head. His body nearly swallowed the stool he was sitting on. He wore a bandanna around his head and a leather jacket with the name "Chopper" embroidered across the back.

Chopper picked something from his teeth. "Did a drywall job there once."

"At the governor's mansion?"

"Yep. The governor's a real nice person. That

job got me back on my feet." He pointed his burrito at the front window. "This highway out front here? Take it east till you come to the cloverleaf."

I nodded. Tobias would know where east was.

"Then head north," he said. "About a mile, mile and a half. Governor's mansion sits on a bluff overlooking the river. You can't miss it. Freaky-looking place with towers and little balconies. Like something straight out of *The Addams Family*."

CHAPTER 13

We'd followed Chopper's directions. We found the governor's mansion and landed in the shrubs in the middle of the circular drive at the front of the house. We demorphed and were now staring at the front door, trying to figure out how to get in.

I peered through a gap in the bushes. Thorn bushes. I hadn't noticed the thorns when I was standing underneath them as a duck. But now I was human, and I noticed.

And Chopper was also right about the place being freaky-looking. Towers and turrets loomed above us. Vines crept up the dark stone walls and circled the stained-glass windows. Pointy black wrought-iron railings lined the balconies and the roof.

"Man. We should've brought our trick-or-treat bags," I said.

<We need to find your governor quickly,> said Ax, <and convince him to speak to us alone. What does he look like?>

"I'm not really sure," I said. "Tobias?"

Tobias blinked his beady hawk eyes.

Ax frowned. <But he is the most important government official in your state. Isn't his picture placed prominently in all your educational facilities?>

"Maybe." I shrugged. "I never really paid much attention." I looked at Tobias.

<Don't ask me,> he said. <My education has taken place mostly outside the established facilities.>

Ax studied Tobias, then me. He shook his head, puzzled. <Perhaps it will not matter. Once we are inside, we will most likely hear someone call him by name.> He narrowed his stalk eyes. <You do know his name?>

Tobias and I looked at each other.

Okay, so I should've done an Internet search before we left the valley. Or picked up a state map at the truck stop. The governor's picture would've been right there on the inside flap, with his name printed underneath.

Or I could've asked Chopper. He would have known.

<So I take it we're back to the finesse thing again?> said Tobias.

I shrugged. "It's been working for us so far."

Except here I couldn't just casually stroll through the door and ask directions. Too much security.

I peeked through the thorns. A tall stone fence, topped with iron spikes and fitted with an alarm system, enclosed the house and grounds. The driveway twisted through a canopy of trees and ended at a gate in the fence. A state trooper manned the guardhouse beside the gate. Another trooper stood watch outside the front door to the mansion. More troopers were probably stationed inside. Not to mention all the maids, cooks, secretaries, and personal assistants we'd have to get past.

Maids, cooks, secretaries, and personal assistants who could be Controllers.

"We use our fly morphs," I said. "Buzz past the guard and into the house. Nobody'll notice us."

<Perfect,> said Tobias, <if we were looking for garbage cans and bathrooms. It's just a guess, but I doubt he'll be spending large amounts of time in either of those places. We could fly around that mausoleum all day and never run into him.>

Ax snorted. <Or recognize him if we did.>

Okay. We deserved that shot. I let it go.

"Well, whatever we do, we have to stay small,"
I said. "We can't let anybody see us except the
governor."

We went over our list of possible morphs.

Rat?

Same problem as the fly, only worse. We'd be
more likely to be seen. And exterminated.

Flea?

Blind and deaf. And not very mobile unless
we caught a ride in somebody's hair. Plus who
wants to put up with the overwhelming need to
suck blood?

"Wolf spiders?" I said.

<People see spiders and go insane,> said To-
bias. <I don't want to end up on the bottom of
somebody's shoe.>

"So . . . what, then? Bat? Chimpanzee? In-
conspicuous, friendly looking Hork-Bajir? What
else have we got?"

<We have a very large black automobile,>
said Ax.

He pointed toward the guardhouse at the end
of the drive. A stretch limo had stopped at the
gate. The guard checked his clipboard and motioned the driver through. The limo crunched up
the winding drive toward us and pulled into the
circle in front of the door. The driver got out, said
something to the guard at the front door, then
stood by the limo, waiting.

"He's not here to pick up the butler," I said. "The governor must be going somewhere."

<Somebody with finesse would probably go with him,> said Tobias.

I nodded. "Yup."

CHAPTER 14

RUN!

It was the only thought in my little cockroach brain: *RUN! OUT OF THE LIGHT! NOW!*

I skittered across the pavement toward the long, dark shadow beneath the limo. Every tiny black hair on my cockroach body trembled. Every nerve cell stood at attention. Two other cockroaches, Ax and Tobias, darted alongside me.

The beauty of being a cockroach — well, relatively speaking — is that suddenly you're Superman. You can be dropped, drowned, blown up. But do you die? No. You simply dust yourself off and scurry away. Get sprayed by a little insecticide? Not a problem. Cockroaches adapt to bug spray. If you are a cockroach, you are nearly inde-structable.

And indestructable was exactly what we needed at the moment.

My six legs motored over chunks of gravel that, to my bug body, were the size of garbage trucks. Through cracks in the pavement that were like canyons. My complex eyes shattered the world around me into thousands of tiny images. But I couldn't stop to piece the picture together. The cockroach recognized light and dark. And it wanted dark.

WOOOOMPH! WOOOOMPH!

The ground quaked.

Footsteps? The cockroach brain didn't have time to wonder. It just propelled my legs. Out of the light. Into the shadow.

Darkness! Yes!

I was under the limo. My nerve cells relaxed. The roach brain released its grip on the crunchy little roach body. But only for a second.

WHAM!

I didn't hear the noise as much as feel it. The roach's body reacted before my human brain had time to register what the sound meant. I shot toward the darkest corner of the shadow.

Ax and Tobias darted behind me. We quivered in the dark.

<Car door?> Tobias.

<That would be my guess,> I said.

WHAM! WHAM!

I jumped. Squeezed into a crack, a corner between the pavement and something big and dark rising up from it. Ax and Tobias huddled beside me.

<If those are car doors,> Ax said, <three of them have now closed. Which means — >

The air exploded around us. Noise. Vibration. Heat.

<It means the driver started the car,> I said. <Let's go! Move, move!>

I scuttled up the vibrating black hulk that towered above me. A rear tire. I climbed, the claws on my feet like spikes gripping into the rubber.

Up. Over. My feet hit metal. And something else. Thick. Sticky. Axle grease. I slogged through it, six tiny feet dragged down with every step. I had to get across it. Had to get to some nonmoving part on the underside of the car. Had to find a safe place to —

<AAAAAAAAAAAHHHHHHHHHH!>

The axle began to move. It was turning. Picking up speed. I clung to it, my feet mired in goo. The axle spun round and round. Faster and faster. Like a washing machine on spin dry.

<AAAAAAAAAAAHHHHHHHHHH!>

Another scream. Not me this time.

77

<Tobias?>

<I'm still on the tire. In a crack in the tread. I think I'm upside down now. No, right side up. No, upside down. Aaaaaaahhhhhhh. Do cockroaches hurrrrrlllll?>

Now that was a good question.

<Is Ax with you?> I said.

<No, I am over here. I do not know where over here is exactly, but it is hot. Very hot. And it is getting hotter. Eeeeee-YOWWWWWWWWWW!>

The limo hurtled down the drive. It probably wasn't going more than twenty miles an hour, but when you're half an inch long, twenty miles an hour might as well be the speed of light. Boulders of gravel pummeled me. The axle spun. The limo jounced up and down over the bumps in the driveway.

And every hair on my cockroach body screamed: GET OUT. TOO MUCH MOVEMENT. TOO MUCH DANGER. RUN!

But my human brain told me to hang on. Hunker down in the grease and wait until it was safe to move.

The spinning and bouncing slowed. The limo rolled to a stop.

<We must be at the gate,> I said. <You've gotta get off the tire, Tobias.>

<Uh, yeah. Tell the driver. He stopped with

me on the bottom. I'm wedged between rubber and pavement.>

The limo edged forward. Stopped again. I heard a whirring noise.

<He's waiting for the gate to open,> I said. <Can you move, Tobias?>

<I already have.> He sidled up beside me in the grease.

Another cockroach — Ax — crawled up behind him. <The bottoms of my feet are numb. I may have fried them completely off.>

<Let's go,> I said. <We don't have much time.>

I scurried along the axle. Ax and Tobias followed. My antennae hit a thick rubber-coated wire hanging down from the underside of the limo. I gripped it with my front claws and scrambled up. Ax followed.

The limo started to roll. The wire swayed. Tobias lunged for it. Caught Ax's back legs instead and hung on.

The limo picked up speed.

<I have a bad feeling about this,> said Tobias.

<We're cool,> I said. <We're cockroaches, remember? Indestructable. Our hearts can stop beating, and we won't die. Our heads can get chopped off, and we still won't die. Well, at least

79

not for a week or so, anyway, until we waste away from thirst and starvation because we don't have a mouths. But hey, that gives us plenty of time to demorph.>

The car swerved. Thumped through a pothole. Our cockroach bodies banged against the underbelly of the limo. Tobias was still hanging from Ax's back legs.

<AAAAAAAAAHHHHHHHHHH!>

We swung back. Banged again. I lost my grip. Twirled around the wire by one leg.

<Forget our hearts and our heads,> Tobias croaked. <If our guts get squashed all over the pavement, it's pretty much over.>

CHAPTER 15

I swung around. Snagged the wire with a second leg. And a third. Pulled my remaining legs in and around.

Ax hung on below me. Tobias scrambled over Ax's back and grasped onto the wire between us.

We clung to it as we shot down the highway at sixty-five miles an hour. Rocks pelted us. Mud puddles drenched us.

Thud-thud-thud-thud. Thud-thud-thud-thud.

The limo thundered through potholes and bumped over metal plates and asphalt patches. We swung from the rubber wire like suicidal trapeze artists.

Thunk.

Banged against the limo above us.

Crunch.

And bounced against the axle below.

<If we get out of here alive,> I said, <I'm writing a letter to the highway department. These roads are terrible.> No one laughed. I guess it wasn't the time for a joke.

The limo slowed again. Turned. Thudded over a speed bump and rolled to a stop.

WHAM!

<Car door,> I said. <We must be wherever we're going. Let's move.>

I dropped to the asphalt. Motored to the edge of the shadow.

<AAAAAAAAAAAAHHHHHHHHHH!>

And was nearly speared by a lady's high heel.

Another high heel extended from the limo and thumped to the pavement beside the first. The governor's wife? I darted toward the pair of heels before she could get away. Scrambled up. Clung to the soft leather as the high heels stepped away from the car.

Suddenly, a man's leg shot from the limo. The governor? Two cockroaches scrambled across the asphalt, over the man's wing tip dress shoe, and up the ankle. Then dove into the cuff of the pant leg.

The other leg emerged, and the Wing Tip escorted the High Heel across the pavement and through a glistening glass door.

They strode across a wide room. A hotel lobby? I hung on, my back end dipping down between thick rug fibers, then flying through the cool air every time High Heel took a step.

<Wherever we are,> I said, <it's someplace nice. The carpet is cushy. And everything gleams. Brass, probably. Marble. Some kind of dark, polished wood.>

A cockroach poked his head up from the cuff of Wing Tip's pant leg. Ax. <And everything smells lemony fresh.>

Wing Tip and High Heel entered another room. Crowded. Noisy. Bright. I'd been in enough of them to guess it was a ballroom, the dance floor in the center, surrounded by tables.

They wound their way through the crowd of people and stopped at a table at the front of the room. Wing Tip pulled out a chair for High Heel, then sat down next to her. A thick white tablecloth draped itself around their legs.

We sat there for a very long time. Human voices murmured and laughed. Dishes and silverware clanked. High Heel crossed and uncrossed her legs several hundred times. Wing Tip dropped his spoon once. He leaned down to get it, and three cockroaches dove for cover.

<Ax, how long have we been in morph?> I said.

<Approximately ninety-seven minutes.>

<Man. We're running out of time, and all these two want to do is eat dinner. Think we can demorph and remorph under the table without anybody noticing?>

The clanks and murmurs quieted. A microphone squealed, and a man's voice boomed through the room. I couldn't make out all the words. Something about being honored and worthy cause and thank you all for coming. I heard clapping, then music erupted from the front of the room.

High Heel pushed her chair back and strode past tables, chairs, waiters. Wing Tip followed. They left the cushy carpet and thumped across a wooden floor.

High heel tapped her toe. Stepped forward. Back. Twirled.

<WHOOOOOOOOOOAAAAAA!>

I twirled, too. By one leg.

In. Out. Forward. Back. We spun round and round. I dug my claws into the leather and hung on. Other feet kicked and stomped around us, inches from my little cockroach head. I scrambled for shelter on the inside of the heel.

The music ended. High Heel stopped spinning.

<Finally,> I said.

But High Heel stayed where she was. The orchestra began playing again. A slow song. She stepped closer to Wing Tip. Her feet swayed. Stayed closer to the ground. Other dancers' feet stayed closer to their own bodies. Away from me.

Except Wing Tip's. His big, gunboats scuffed up against High Heel's gray pumps. Trounced on her toes. I hid on the inside of her heel, under her instep. About the fourth time he mashed her foot, she kicked his shin. I was starting to like this woman.

Ax's head poked up from the tweed cuff. <One hundred and six minutes have passed.>

<So, what, that gives us fourteen minutes?> I scanned the sea of legs around us. <We can't demorph on the dance floor.>

Wing Tip trounced again. I dove for cover. High Heel gave him another swift kick, turned and strode away. She wove her way across the ballroom, through chairs and dessert carts. Wing Tip and two sets of men's plain black dress shoes followed.

A door opened, and we entered another room. Smaller. Darker. Quieter. A conference room. The door closed, and both sets of black dress shoes positioned themselves in front of it. High Heel sat in the chair at the end of the long conference table. Wing Tip paced.

"I hate this," he said. "Smiling. Shaking hands. Begging for campaign contributions. Makes me feel like a dancing poodle."

Campaign contributions? That's all I needed to hear. Wing Tip was definitely the governor.

And it was show time.

CHAPTER 16

Ax and Tobias stayed hidden in the tweed cuff. I crawled down the high heel and into the thick carpet under the conference table.

I began to demorph.

My roach body swelled. Up, then out. Like a crunchy brown beach ball. The shattered image of table legs and gray high heels smoothed into one unified picture as my compound roach eyes melded into two human eyes.

<Governor.> My thought-speak rang out. <You might want to sit down. You're about to see something that will scare the pee out of you.>

Silence.

Then: "Who said that?"

"I don't see anybody."

87

"Is there a microphone in here? Speakers?"

A woman's voice. "I thought you said this room was secure, Frank."

I dragged my bloated body across the carpet. Out from under the table, where I could see . . . and be seen.

<Please be careful, Marco.> Ax's thought-speak was no more than a whisper.

As I grew, I kept a close eye on the people in the room. The dress shoes turned out to be two plainclothes security guys. Pistol handles bulged beneath their suit jackets.

Wing Tip was tall. Distinguished. Like a TV news guy. Chiseled cheek bones. Aristocratic nose. Perfectly styled hair, fashionably gray at the temples.

High Heel was just the opposite, short and plump. Everything about her was frumpy, lumpy, and gray. Her dress. Her shoes. Even her face. Everything but her eyes. Gray, yes. But a quick, intelligent gray.

She turned those eyes on me. On the black lump of boy/insect growing from the carpet.

And pulled back in horror. Maybe even revulsion.

"Frank?"

She spoke to Wing Tip, but kept her eyes on me. Watched four of my legs bulge into human legs and arms, the other two shrivel away into nothing.

Wing Tip followed her gaze. A strangled cry bubbled up from his throat. "Omigod." He grabbed one of the security guards by the arm and shoved him toward me.

Both security guys stared. Reached for their guns.

<Governor!> My sideways cockroach mouth melted into lips, teeth, and tongue. "Governor!" I was human now. I stepped toward Wing Tip, my hands in the air. "Tell them not to shoot. Please."

"No. Don't shoot. Just watch him. Closely."

It was an order. But it didn't come from Wing Tip. It came from High Heel.

I turned.

"I am the governor," she said. Her face was white, her body tense. But her eyes remained steady. "And who are you?"

The governor? I stared at her. It didn't even occur to me that the governor could be a woman.

<I won't tell Rachel if you won't,> said Tobias.

"I — I'm an Animorph," I said.

A sharp intake of breath. One of the security guards? I glanced toward the door, where the two of them stood in front of Wing Tip. Was one of them a Controller? Both of them?

The governor frowned. "Excuse me? An Ani — what?"

"I'm one of the good guys."

I still had my hands in the air. I lowered them. Slowly. Took a step toward her. Mustered up all my charm. My sincerity. My finesse.

Click. Click.

I heard the security guys release the safety catches on their pistols. I kept my eyes on the governor.

"You have to believe me," I told her. "The entire state — no, the entire planet — depends on it. And you're the only one who can help."

The governor studied me. "Flattery, huh? Okay, I'm listening."

I watched the security guards. The tall one stood open-mouthed. The pistol in his hand trembled. He clearly wanted to run screaming from the room.

But the short one glared at me, his finger steady on the trigger of his gun. Hatred twisted his face.

"That guard." I pointed at the short guy. "That guard is not going to follow your orders, Governor. He's going to shoot me. Then he'll probably shoot you, too. And your husband. And the other security guard."

"Don't be ridiculous," said the governor. "His job is to protect me. He won't shoot you unless I tell him to. Or unless you attack me. In fact, he'll take his itchy little finger off the trigger right now." She watched the short guard until he did as she said. "And Collins?" She looked at the other guard. "Make sure he keeps it off."

Collins nodded. He backed up a step toward the door, obviously relieved to be watching another security guard instead of the amazing Roach Boy.

If he only knew the horror that was wrapped around Short Guy's brain.

"Ax? Tobias?" I said.

Two cockroaches crawled from Wing Tip's cuff, down his ankle, and over his shoe. One of the roaches began growing. The other turned blue, then it ballooned out, too.

Quietly. Inconspicuously. Nobody noticed them at first, two enormous mutant insects half hidden behind Wing Tip's legs. Tobias's exoskeleton melted into his bulging body, and feathers popped out. Ax's claws turned into hands and Andalite hooves.

Tobias spread his wings and flapped onto a lampshade in the corner of the room.

"Oh!" Collins gawked. "But . . . where . . . ?"

"A hawk?" The governor stared at him. Stared at me. Frowned.

"Yes. A hawk!" Short Guy leveled his pistol at Tobias.

Then he saw Ax. Tall. Blue. Almost completely demorphed.

"Andalite!"

Short Guy whirled. Aimed.

"NO!"

I dove. Missed. Short Guy squeezed the trigger. Collins knocked the pistol upward.

BLAM!

The paneling above Ax's head shattered.

Fwap.

Ax nailed Short Guy with his tail blade. Held him against the wall.

Collins stared at Ax. "Who . . . wha . . . ?"

<His firearm,> Ax ordered.

Collins nodded. Pulled the pistol from Short Guy's hand. Backed away.

Tromped on Wing Tip's foot.

Wing Tip shoved him aside. "Idiot." He leaned down to rub the footprint from the top of his shoe.

"Okay, now if everybody can stay calm, we've got a little story to tell." I looked at the governor. "It might take a while."

The governor considered this for a moment. Studied me. Studied Ax. Studied Short Guy.

She turned to Wing Tip. "Go back in to the ballroom. Make my apologies. Tell everyone I'm not feeling well. Assure them it's nothing serious. A cold or something." She glanced at me. Narrowed her eyes. "And Frank? Don't say anything else."

Wing Tip nodded and slipped out the door.

I watched him leave. He seemed so calm under the circumstances.

Yeah. Too calm. Any normal person would have been amazed, fascinated, creeped out. Wing Tip hadn't even been shocked by a full-fledged Andalite. I glanced at Collins and the governor. They were still staring at Ax's stalk eyes, deadly tail and mouthless face.

But Wing Tip had been more concerned with wiping Collins's footprint off his shoe. As if a four-legged alien were nothing unusual. Nothing new.

Nothing he hadn't seen before.

"Governor," I said, "we have to move. Fast. Tobias? Firepower. Now."

93

CHAPTER 17

Tobias swooped from the lampshade and landed on the carpet. Blades began to erupt from his feathers.

I concentrated. Focused on the gorilla.

Too late!

The door burst open. Wing Tip barreled through, followed by four waiters wielding Dracon beams.

"Hork-Bajir!"

Wing Tip pointed at Tobias, now almost fully morphed. One of the Controllers leveled his Dracon at Tobias's leathery gut. Tobias dove.

TSSSSEEEEEEEEWWWWWWW!

The conference table sizzled in two. Both halves dropped to the floor.

"Oh!" The governor stared at the smoldering wood. Then at her husband. "Frank! What are you — ?"

A Controller grabbed her.

Tobias vaulted over the pieces of the table.

WHACK!

Struck the Controller with his wrist blade.

"AAAAAAAAAAHHHHHHHH!"

The Controller screamed. Dropped the governor. Stared at his fingerless hand.

The other Controllers charged. Tobias sliced. Ax's tail lashed out.

FWAP! FWAP!

I was fully morphed, fully gorilla now. I stormed through flying bullets, blades, and Dracon beams.

Collins had crawled to the governor and was shielding her with his body. He held his pistol with both hands, aiming first at a Controller, then at Tobias, then at Ax, not sure what or who to shoot.

TSSSSEEEEEEEEWWWWWWW!

"AAAAAAAAAHHHHHH!"

Dracon fire seared Collins's shoulder. Blasted a hole in the wall behind him.

<Go!> I told him. <NOW! There's nothing you can do here. Governor! Time to bail!>

I wrapped one gorilla arm around her.

Wing Tip reached for her. "Honey! Take my hand. I'll save you."

95

The governor grabbed a chair and swung it over her head. I thought she was aiming at me. I ducked.

CRASH!

Wing Tip crumpled to the floor.

"Save me, huh?" she said with a frown.

I leaped over Wing Tip's motionless body. <Let's go, let's go!> I yelled at Ax and Tobias.

"Collins!" the governor cried.

I turned. Collins lay on the carpet, stunned, his shoulder a lump of charred meat.

I grabbed him in my free arm and leaped through the smoke and chaos. Charged through the door. Into the ballroom. Ax and Tobias bounded after me.

"AAAAAAAA!"

"Omigod!"

Women screamed. Men screamed. Chairs, dishes, serving trays crashed to the floor as the well-dressed crowd scrambled for the doors.

A waiter charged forward. Leveled a Dracon at the governor.

"No!" Collins.

He aimed his pistol.

BLAM!

"AAAAAAAAAAAAAHHHHHHHH!"

The waiter fell, blood gushing from his thigh.

Collins collapsed against me. I rolled him under a table. Pulled the heavy tablecloth down to hide him.

<Stay here till the smoke clears,> I said. <Don't even try to be a hero.>

"There! Get them!"

Wing Tip's voice! I whirled. Controllers burst from the conference room.

"Don't let them take the governor," yelled Wing Tip. "Kill her if you have to."

The governor stared at him. "What is he saying?"

<Don't worry,> I said. <We'll get you out.>

Wing Tip and his buddies charged from behind. More Controllers streamed through the ballroom doors and beat their way through the fleeing crowd.

<Service entrance!> Tobias directed.

He bolted toward a tangle of waiters pushing through a small door at the front of the ballroom. I knuckle-walked after him. Knocked over a huge coffee pot. Hurdled a dessert cart. Ax followed. Across the dance floor. Around the orchestra pit.

A Controller leaped from behind a bass drum.

I grabbed a tuba. Shoved it over his head.

Tobias reached the door, shoved the waiters aside and crashed through. I followed. Down a short hallway. Into the kitchen.

A state trooper and a guy in a chauffeur's uniform were sitting at a small table, munching party food and playing poker with the chef.

Tobias vaulted over them.

"Wha — ?" The trooper half rose from his chair. Fumbled with the holster of his pistol.

I barreled past, the governor tucked under my arm.

"Governor!" The chauffeur scrambled to his feet. "Where are you going, ma'am?"

"I'm not sure," she called back.

TSSSSEEEEEEEEWWWWWWW!

Dracon fire blasted through the kitchen.

Fwap. Fwap-fwap.

I heard Ax behind me, his hooves clicking on the tile floor, his tail striking again and again.

We kept going. Around waiters, busboys, cooks. The pastry chef pulled a Dracon beam from his jacket and leveled it at the governor. She flattened him with a cutting board.

We slammed through one set of doors. Then another. Finally, outside. Around a Dumpster. Across the loading dock.

<Limo!> Tobias bounded toward the long black car parked by the dock, the same limo that had brought us here. <Doors unlocked. Keys inside! Oh come on. This is *way* too easy.>

TSSSSEEEEEEEEWWWWWWW!

The concrete exploded beneath my feet.

I swung over the side of the dock. Ripped open the back door of the limo. Dumped the governor inside.

<Sorry. I have better manners when Yeerks aren't shooting at me.> I jumped in after her. <Keep your head down.>

Tobias squeezed into the driver's seat. Banged his wrist blade into the tinted window that divided· the front seat from the back. The glass shattered.

<Ooops.>

He folded his knees under the steering wheel, his arms around it. His neck was twisted over, the side of his leathery Hork-Bajir face crushed against the top of the limo.

<Not comfy,> he said.

But also not a problem for a guy with blades growing from his skull.

Thump. Scuuuuurrrrr-UUUUNNNCH.

He tore through the top of the limo like he was opening a tin can. <Sun roof.>

He poked his head through the hole, cranked the key, and the limo revved to life.

<Ax!> I yelled. <Let's go!>

Ax downed two Controllers, clattered across the loading zone, and leaped into the backseat of the limo. I yanked the door shut.

<GO! GO! GO!>

Tobias floored it. We screeched across the parking lot and into the street.

We had now added yet another kidnapping to our crimes.

CHAPTER 18

We squealed across four lanes of traffic. Thundered up over the curb on the other side.

Dropped back down onto the pavement. Sideswiped a delivery truck. In. Out. Around. Weaving through cars, trucks, SUVs. All I could see of Tobias were his shoulders and elbows. His head jutted up through the hole in the roof.

I bounced along on the rear seat. Watched out the back and side windows, my gorilla skull thump-thump-thumping against the ceiling of the limo. The governor sat in the seat opposite, trying not to slide back and forth as the limo careened first left, then right. Her fingers dug into the leather armrest on the door beside her.

Ax struggled to gain a foothold on the floor in

101

between the banks of seats. He gazed at the governor. His Andalite eyes radiated warmth and . . . joy.

Yes, joy. We were doing ninety in heavy traffic with clumsy Hork-Bajir hands at the wheel, and Ax looked like he'd just found the secret to inner peace.

<Madam Governor.> He bowed low. Stretched his front leg out in front of him. His head nearly touched the floor. <I am Aximili-Esgarrouth-Isthill, and I am honored to be in the presence of a great leader.>

"A great leader?" The governor thumped against the side of the limo as Tobias screeched sideways into a bank parking lot. "Me?"

Ax nodded. <I only regret that our meeting was not under less difficult circumstances.>

Difficult. Yeah. Okay. Tobias plowed around the bank. Through the drive-up lane.

Over a curb. For three full seconds, the limo was airborne —

WOOOOMPH!

— before slamming down onto a side street. Tobias screeched sideways and kept going.

"Aaaahhhlllp!" The governor swallowed a scream. She managed to wrench her right hand free from the armrest and hold it out to Ax.

He shook it, then bowed low again. <I will guard your life with my own.>

"Very reassuring," she said.

The limo hurdled a median strip.

The governor gripped the armrest. "I mean that sincerely, Aximili."

<As do I, Governor.>

<And Jake thought you were the one with charm, Marco,> Tobias said dryly.

<Just keep your eyes on the road,> I said. <And I don't ever want to hear another word of criticism about *my* driving.>

The limo skidded around a corner. Leveled a row of newspaper vending machines.

A police siren! Red and blue lights flashed behind us.

<Trouble,> I said.

<You think?> Tobias.

I turned. More sirens. More flashing red and blue lights ahead. Three, maybe four cars.

Tobias jerked the wheel. We slid sideways into a pickup. Tobias gunned the engine, and we shot down an alley, the pickup's bumper trailing from ours.

The limo thundered through potholes. Around Dumpsters. Shot across the next side street and into the alley in the next block.

<Oh, man!>

The brakes squealed. I plunged forward, then slammed back against the seat. Ax crashed into my lap.

"Ooomph."

<Hey, watch the tail!>

The limo had stopped nose to nose with a trash truck. The governor was sprawled on the floor. She struggled to pull herself back onto the seat.

TSSSSEEEEEEEEWWWWWWW!

Dracon fire shattered the window next to where the she'd been sitting. Incinerated the headrest that had been behind her.

<Stay down, Governor! On the floor!>

She nodded. Stared up at the smoldering headrest. "No arguments here."

She pulled her knees up to her chest, wrapped her skirt and her arms around them, and hunkered down between the seats. Her face had lost all color, but her eyes were still bright. Steady.

Tobias threw the limo in reverse and started to back up.

A police car turned into the alley behind us.

BAM! BAM!

Gunfire!

Ax and I hit the deck again and crouched beside the governor.

Tobias threw the limo in drive. We lurched forward. Squeezed past the trash truck. The right wheels thumped over the bottom two steps of a concrete stairway leading up to a loading dock.

SssccccuuurrrRRREEEEEEEEE.

We scraped against the trash truck on one side, the loading dock on the other.

And spit through into the alley beyond. A police car screamed into the narrow opening ahead. Came barreling toward us!

Tobias gunned the engine. Sideswiped the police car and shot out into the street!

Cranked the wheel. Dodged oncoming traffic. Sped the wrong way down the one-way street, warehouses towering above us on one side, the riverbank dropping away from us on the other, chased by an army of sirens and flashing lights. City police, county deputies, state troopers.

Some of them were Controllers. Some probably weren't. But it didn't matter. As far as the non-Controllers were concerned, lunatic monsters had kidnapped their governor. They were as determined as the Controllers to stop us.

THWOK! THWOK! THWOK! THWOK!

I looked up. A helicopter thundered overhead. I could see it through the sun roof. The real sun roof, not Tobias's emergency hatch. The pilot pitched the helicopter forward in a steep dive. Sunlight glinted off something in the passenger door.

A Dracon beam.

The governor saw it, too.

"Time to ditch the limo," she said. "We're too

big. Too easy to spot. We'll have a better chance on foot."

Good thinking. Behind those alert gray eyes lurked the brain of a combat general.

<I know the perfect place,> said Tobias. <Get ready to bail.>

An intersection loomed ahead. A main thoroughfare crossed our one-way street and led to a bridge.

Tobias floored it and quickly turned the wheel. The limo skidded around the corner and hurtled onto the bridge. He slammed on the brakes and the limo screeched sideways. Plowed into a concrete pillar and lurched to a stop, blocking traffic from both directions.

Cars honked. Skidded. Slammed into each other.

Tobias dove from the driver's door. I threw the governor over Ax's back, flung the back door open, and we ran out into the chaos.

CHAPTER 19

<Let's go, let's go!>

Tobias bounded up over the hood of a sports car. I followed. Leaping from hood to roof to trunk. From car to truck to minivan. Over a jack-knifed eighteen-wheeler.

Ax stayed on the ground and galloped between the vehicles. The governor hugged his shoulders and squeezed her knees into his sides to keep from falling off.

Police cars skidded onto the bridge behind us. Cops streamed from the cars and barricaded themselves behind the limo, weapons drawn.

<Stay low!> I shouted.

I leaped from the top of an SUV to the back of a jeep.

The jeep's driver climbed from the front. Stared at his crumpled bumper. Cursed, kicked his tire, and started punching numbers on his cell phone.

I vaulted over him.

He stared at me. "Oh my . . . oh my . . . AAAAAAAAAHHHH!" He tossed the phone to the road and sprinted toward the other end of the bridge.

BAM! BAM!

Bullets whizzed past. Bounced off steel and concrete.

Drivers screamed and dove under their cars.

I dropped and hugged the ground. Tobias crouched beside me. Ax skidded behind a UPS truck, the governor still on his back.

A man's voice boomed out over bridge. "Hold your fire. HOLD. YOUR. FIRE. They've got the governor. And innocent motorists are trapped on that bridge."

Thank God. The guy with the bullhorn was a legitimate, uninfested cop. With a brain.

BAM! BAM BAM!

But the Controllers obviously weren't taking orders from the sane guy.

I walked between cars. Tobias followed and Ax, still carrying the governor, galloped behind.

"They're getting away!"

"After them!"

Cops swarmed over the limo. Raced across the bridge behind us.

<Go go go!> I yelled. <We can make it. We're closer to the other end of the bridge than the cops are to us!>

THWOK! THWOK! THWOK! THWOK!

The helicopter was back. It hovered over the bridge, just above the tall suspension cables.

More sirens! Flashing lights. Not from behind this time, but from in front. Police cars screamed onto the other end of the bridge. Cops leaped from the patrol cars.

We dove for the pavement again. Crouched low between a Frito delivery truck and a TV repair van.

TSSSSEEEEEEEEWWWWWWW!

The delivery truck exploded. Fritos rained down on us as we rolled under the van.

TSSSSEEEEEEEEWWWWWWW!

A concrete pillar in front of the van shattered into dust.

SSSCCCUUUUURRRRENNNNCH.

The steel beam it had been holding swayed. The suspension cable whipped through the air.

"AAAAAAAAAAHHHHHHHHH!"

The remaining motorists fled from their cars and ran screaming toward both ends of the bridge.

I inched out from under the van. Raised my

head. Cops in front. Cops behind. Chopper over-head.

And below us, the river.

A few barges in the distance. Some fishing boats. And a sailboat. Did I say sailboat? Make that a yacht, slowly cruising toward us.

<You scared of heights, Governor?> I said.

"As opposed to what? Bullets? Laser beams that vaporize solid concrete? A bridge that might collapse under me at any moment?" She shook her head. Took a deep breath. "Let's do it."

"Let's do it?" A vision flashed into my head, the governor when she was a kid. She looked like . . . Rachel?

I shook the image from my mind. <You heard the governor. Let's do it.>

I pulled her from under the van and climbed onto the bridge rail.

The yacht skimmed through the water. I could hear music and laughter. Could see people crowded on the deck. A party.

The boat neared the bridge. Close. Closer.

NOW!

I wrapped one massive gorilla arm tight around the governor and leaped into space.

CHAPTER 20

We dropped. Straight down.

The governor held on tight. She dug her fingers into my fur and didn't even scream. Not even a whimper.

I liked this lady.

Down, down we fell. The yacht loomed larger and larger. I kept a tight grip on the governor with one arm. When we were close enough, I reached out with the other and grabbed the yacht's mast in my gorilla fist and hung on.

The mast bowed, groaned, and bent almost double. The sail beat against me. My feet brushed the bow of the boat, then bounded into the air again as the mast sprang back and we swung over the cabin.

I spun around. Gripped the bottom of the mast with my fingerlike toes and held tight.

The yacht slid under the bridge. The music and laughter continued. Party guests danced. Munched crackers. Refilled their drinks. They didn't even notice the gorilla hanging from the sail, clutching their governor in one arm like a rag doll.

Didn't even notice the Hork-Bajir drop over the edge of the bridge above them. A strange, shrinking Hork-Bajir, sprouting feathers. Tobias. His blades shriveled. His serpent neck receded into his bird body. Just before he hit the water, his arms melted into wings. He flapped hard and just skimmed over the surface of the river.

Ax dropped from the bridge behind him, his Andalite body sharply outlined against the setting sun. He kicked. Flailed.

Kuh-SPLAT!

Belly-flopped into the river and sank.

I waited. Saw nothing. No stalk eyes peaking above the surface. No tail blade slicing through the water.

<Ax? Ax!>

The governor scanned the river. "Can Aximili swim?"

<Yeah.>

We watched. Searched the waves. Still no Ax.

"We have to do something," the governor

112

said. "The impact could have broken his legs. Or his ribs. Maybe knocked him unconscious!"

<There!> Tobias tipped his wing.

A dorsal fin broke the surface of the water and skimmed alongside the yacht.

My heart started beating again.

<Hey, Ax-man. Glad you could make it. He's fine,> I told the governor. I motioned toward the fin. <He morphed a shark.>

"Morphed . . . a shark." The governor nodded. "That's good. I think."

The yacht had cleared the bridge and was sailing in open water.

I slid down the mast, vaulted over the cabin and onto the top deck.

"Wha — ?" The yacht's captain backed up. Stared at us.

I leaped over the rail and onto the hors d'oeuvres table. Left a giant gorilla footprint in a bowl of bean dip.

And landed in the middle of the party.

"AAAAAAAAAHHHHHHHH!"

The party guests screamed and scrambled to safety. A woman backed up against the railing and toppled, head over heels, into the river.

"I can't swim! Somebody help. I can't swim!"

Tobias swooped over the yacht, plucked a life jacket from the deck and tossed it out to her. She grabbed hold.

113

A dorsal fin broke the surface of the water behind her as Ax nudged the woman to shore.

All while cops raced from the bridge and along the banks.

"There!" A Controller motioned to the helicopter. "On the boat!"

The helicopter dove after us.

THWOK! THWOK! THWOK! THWOK!

The downdraft from the rotors whipped the water into waves. The yacht pitched and rolled.

The party-goers screamed even louder. Grabbed onto the railings and deck chairs to keep from being tossed overboard.

The helicopter hovered now. A Controller leaned from the passenger door, weapon in hand.

<Get down!> I screamed. <Everybody!>

I dropped to the deck. Rolled the governor under a table.

Tobias circled above. Zeroed in on the Controller's outstretched arm and dove.

The Controller spotted him. Beat him away with the Dracon beam. Then took quick aim.

TSEEEEEWWW-ka-BLOOOOOOSH!

"OH MY GOD! WHAT WAS THAT?"

"ARE THEY CRAZY?"

"HELP! SOMEBODY HELP US! PLEASE!"

TSEEEEEWWW-ka-BLOOOOOOSH!

Another shot! The water boiled. The yacht reeled.

The party-goers shrieked and scrambled to the back of the boat. Pushed each other aside and clambered over the railing and leaped into the water. Even the yacht's captain abandoned ship. He dove from the top deck into the river.

It was madness.

Police cars sped along the riverbanks, guns and Dracons blazing.

Party-goers bobbed in the water, a sea of arms and legs, life jackets and fancy clothes, splashing and struggling toward shore.

The captainless yacht spun wildly, forced downstream by the current.

The governor crawled from under the wet bar.

<No!> I said. <Stay down.>

"Somebody has to pilot this boat. We'll capsize. Or run aground. We're too close to shore."

<Oh. Okay.>

The governor climbed up onto the second deck and grabbed the wheel. The boat stopped spinning. The bow straightened and turned. We headed toward open river.

The helicopter banked and circled for another shot.

On deck I grabbed pitchers and margarita glasses and hurled them at the helicopter. Specifically, at the Controller with the Dracon.

Hey, you use what weapons you have.

TSSSSEEEEEEEEWWWWWWW!

A deck chair disintegrated.

I flung a bottle. It clanked off the glass bubble in front of the pilot. The chopper dipped and rocked.

Then it straightened and pitched forward in a steep dive.

THWOK! THWOK! THWOK!

The helicopter hovered now only a few feet above my head. The noise was deafening. The downdraft churned the water and whipped chairs and life preservers around the deck. I held tight to the railing to steady myself as the boat pitched and rocked.

The Controller leaned from the helicopter and steadied his Dracon against the hull.

Tobias! I saw him flap to gain altitude. Turn. Dive!

Too late!

TSSSSEEEEEEEEWWWWWWW!

Ka-BOOM!

The bow of the yacht exploded.

CHAPTER 21

Chunks of fiberglass pelted my hide. Smoke burned my nose and lungs.

I coughed. Brushed debris from my face.

<Governor?>

No answer. The yacht tipped. The bow glugged then slipped beneath the waves. The stern shot from the water into the air.

I wedged my feet against the wet bar to keep from sliding toward the bow. Pulled my face level with the top deck. The wheel was already submerged, a gaping hole blown into the deck beneath it. Water lapped at the shattered wood and poured into the cabin below.

<Governor!>

<Marco! Watch out!>

117

I turned. Tobias hurtled toward the helicopter. The Controller leaned from the door, Dracon beam leveled at the sinking boat. At me.

Tobias zeroed in. Raked his talons forward.

Nailed him!

The Dracon plummeted toward the river.

Tobias dove. Nabbed the Dracon beam in midair and lobbed it to me.

I gripped it in one gorilla hand. Raised my arm. Aimed. The pilot saw me and his face twisted in terror. The helicopter whipped up and around.

And jetted away.

I waited until he was down river, away from the yacht. Then I held my arm steady and squeezed the trigger.

TSSSSEEEEEEEEWWWWWWW!

Ka-BOOOOOOM!

The helicopter burst into flames. Thick black smoke rolled over the river.

I hurled the Dracon beam into the water.

<Gotta bail, Marco.> Tobias swooped overhead. <Let's go, let's go!>

<You go,> I shouted. <You and Ax. I have to find the governor!>

I climbed over the wet bar. Ripped the cabin door open and crawled inside. Waded into the murky water that filled the cabin.

The governor had fallen through from the deck above. She was slumped facedown across a table, submerged to her waist. Her gray dress floated around her. Her wet gray curls lay plastered against her skull. I turned her over. Blood streamed from a gash on her forehead.

<Governor.> I felt for a pulse. <Can you hear me?>

Her eyelids flickered. She nodded weakly. "I'll be okay."

I pulled her from the water, hoisted her onto my back, and climbed from the submerged cabin.

The yacht listed sharply now, the stern standing nearly straight in the air. The wreck of the helicopter burned downriver. Black, choking smoke engulfed us.

<Marco!> Ax circled the sinking yacht. <We are seriously running out of time.>

<They're bringing in speedboats,> said Tobias. <I can see them on the highway. Let's go!>

I lay the governor over the wet bar. She gripped the rail behind her and struggled to sit up.

I was already demorphing. Gorilla hands shrank to human hands. Gorilla fur melted into human skin.

The boat groaned. Water crept over my ankles. My knees.

119

My jaw pushed back and my nose pushed forward. Arms shrank. Legs grew. I stood upright. I was human.

But I wasn't finished.

"Governor." My face shot out into a bottlenose. "How do you feel about marine mammals?"

The governor stared at the fin growing from my back. "Well, I wouldn't marry one." She managed a weak smile.

My head and neck melted into one streamlined unit. Legs fused into a tail. Arms shrank to flippers. Two hundred extra teeth erupted from my jaws.

The water edged over the cabin door and lapped at the wet bar. The governor climbed onto the back rail.

Tobias swooped overhead. <Ticktock, Marco. Ticktock.>

My skin thickened and faded to a light bluish gray. Finally, I flopped into the water. I was a dolphin.

I floated above the sinking yacht. The governor straddled my back and held tight to my dorsal fin. Together we slid through the water, through the smoke and confusion of the helicopter blast.

And the yacht sank into the river.

CHAPTER 22

The governor stared at me. "Parasitic aliens are invading Earth." She kept her voice even. "And my husband is controlled by one."

I nodded. "Yeah. Basically, that's the story."

"Thank God." She sank back into her leather chair and ran her hand through her damp gray curls. "I was beginning to think something much, much worse was happening. Aliens we can fight."

She refilled her coffee mug from the pot on her desk. We were in her office on the top floor of the governor's mansion. We'd bolted the door and shoved a heavy bookcase in front of it. Ax stood guard, tail poised. Tobias was perched on a windowsill, watching the back of the mansion.

121

Posted at the other window, watching the front, was Collins.

Yes, Collins.

We'd found him in the bathroom off the governor's office. He was crouched in the tub waiting for the governor to return, his charred shoulder wrapped in the shower curtain. Ax and I helped him out into the office, and the governor cleaned and bandaged the wound as best she could.

Now she sat at her desk, slugging down cup after cup of coffee. She'd changed into sweats and a snazzy pair of Nikes. Her gray fund-raising dress lay in a soggy mound on the bathroom floor, and she'd lost her high heels somewhere between the limo and the yacht. She paged through her day planner and scribbled names and phone numbers on a pad.

I sat across from her, studying a roster of National Guard officers. I slid it across the desk.

"Call every officer on this list," I said. "Some of them will be Controllers. Some won't. But if you can get enough non-Controllers to listen to you, Visser One's operation will collapse."

<For now, anyway,> said Tobias.

The governor nodded, picked up the phone, and punched in the number of the first name on the roster. General Sherman, the commander of the Army National Guard.

"I want all units to stand down," she told him. "Take no action whatsoever. None. Yes, that's a direct order. From your commander in chief, that's who."

She slammed the phone down.

<He resisted orders from his commander?> Ax glanced at me. <He must be a Controller.>

"Maybe. Maybe not," said the governor. "He's a cantankerous old coot who can't stand taking orders from a woman. He doesn't need an alien wrapped around his brain to make him hard to get along with. Okay, who's next?" She ran her finger down the roster. "The commander of the Air National Guard."

She punched in the number and gave the air commander the same orders she'd given General Sherman. Then she phoned the next officer, and the next, making her way down the roster.

I paced from window to window to bathroom to desk. Even fixed myself a cup of coffee, heavy on the sugar and nondairy creamer.

"Ugh."

It tasted like motor oil. Creamy, sweet motor oil. I shuddered and set the cup on the windowsill.

The governor hung up the phone. Ran her finger down the list to the next officer. And froze.

"Lieutenant Colonel Larsen." She stared at the name. "His battalion just rolled back into town this morning. They've been on a military exercise in the desert." A slow smile spread over her face. "For the past two weeks."

"Two weeks?" I blinked. "That means —"

<It means we've got an entire battalion of certified Yeerk-free soldiers,> said Tobias.

The governor nodded. "Roughly six hundred troops."

"This is . . . this is great." I pushed the phone toward her. "Call him. Tell him to keep his troops together. Have them bunker down someplace where the Yeerks can't get to them."

"I think I know just the place."

She took the phone from me and punched in a number.

"Colonel Larsen?" she said. "This is the governor. And I've got a little emergency."

The call took about a minute and a half. The governor told the lieutenant colonel what she needed, and the lieutenant colonel's voice boomed back through the receiver. "Yes, Ma'am."

She hung up. "We're converting the grounds of the governor's mansion into temporary headquarters. Colonel Larsen's battalion can set up camp on the lawn." She shook her head. "My gardener's going to have a stroke."

The governor ran her finger down the list and punched in the next number. She called every officer on the roster, then pushed the phone aside.

"Well. I guess that's it. We've done everything we can do."

"Not quite," I said. "You're a target now. You need some personal security. Bodyguards."

"I've got Collins," said the governor.

"That's good, and no offense, Collins." I shot him an apologetic smile. "But —"

"But one security guard with a bad shoulder isn't gonna do it," he said. "I'll do everything I can, Governor. You know that. But you need more people."

I nodded. Looked at the governor. "Can you think of anybody else? Somebody you can count on? Somebody who can keep you safe? Is there anyone that you know for sure has been far away, maybe even out of the country, for more than three days?"

The governor frowned. Rifled through her day planner. "Yes!" She tapped her finger on a page. "Major MacDonald. Deputy director of the state police. He just got back from a week-long Interpol conference in Paris, and I think he took a couple of other officers with him."

She picked up the phone, punched a number, and told MacDonald what she needed.

"He's on his way," she said as she hung up. "He lives on this side of town, so it shouldn't take long."

"I hope not," said Collins.

He pushed the heavy drapes aside so we could see.

"We got company, Governor."

Yes, we certainly did.

A column of Humvees and military trucks were rolling up the highway.

CHAPTER 23

The lead Humvee was about a mile away. The line of military vehicles behind it stretched over the next hill.

"Any chance that's Colonel Larsen's battalion?" I said.

The governor shook her head. "He hasn't had time to muster his troops. They won't be here for hours." She peered through the window. "Besides, this unit's too small. I count six Humvees and eight trucks. Maybe a couple more at the back that we can't see. It's not big enough for a battalion." She frowned. "But I didn't order any other units to report here."

Ax watched the convoy. <If those troops are

not following the governor's orders, they must be following someone else's.> He turned his stalk eyes toward me.

"Yeah," I said. "Visser One. Governor, we have to get you out of here. Fast. We'll go out the back. Use the river again."

<Don't think so.>

Tobias motioned his head toward the back window. Police boats patroled the river beneath the mansion.

"Great." I stared at the boats. Then at the convoy. "There's gotta be a way out."

A siren wailed. I turned. A police car screamed down the highway from the opposite direction, lights flashing.

"Geez, Governor." Collins's voice edged toward panic. "They're coming at us from all sides."

"No." I watched the police car speed toward us. "Not this one. The Yeerks wouldn't send one car by itself."

The governor nodded. "MacDonald. It has to be MacDonald."

<Let's hope he gets here before the Humvees do,> said Tobias.

The convoy rolled down the highway, half a mile from the mansion. The police car hurtled toward it, a streak of red and blue.

The governor picked up the phone. Made one more call. This time to the guardhouse.

"Open the gate," she said. "A state police car will be approaching in a matter of seconds. Let it through. Don't stop it. I repeat. Do not stop it. I've given the police officer clearance."

The turnoff to the the governor's mansion lay in a dip between two hills. A Humvee topped the hill on the convoy side. The police car flew over the hill opposite. It streaked over the last stretch of highway and squealed into the turnoff, spraying dust and gravel over the Humvee.

Then the car shot through the open gate, barreled up the drive, and skidded to a stop at the front entrance to the mansion. The doors banged open. Three officers leaped out.

"That's him. The tall one." The governor pointed. "MacDonald."

The officers bolted inside. Seconds later, footsteps thundered down the hall. We shoved the bookcase aside and unlocked the door. MacDonald burst into the office, followed by the other two police officers. I bolted the door behind them.

"Ma'am." MacDonald nodded at the governor. His gaze swept over the other occupants of the room. Me, your average good-looking kid. Collins, one shoulder inexpertly bandaged. The hawk on the windowsill. MacDonald frowned and shook his head.

And Ax.

"Ahhh!"

MacDonald reached for his pistol.

"No!" The governor grabbed his arm. "This is Aximili-Esgarrouth-Isthill. He's an Andalite. A friend."

Ax stepped forward and bowed his head. Kept his stalk eyes on MacDonald's pistol and his tail blade poised.

MacDonald narrowed his eyes. Studied Ax. His hand hovered near his holster.

"I'll explain everything when we have more time," the governor said. "Right now you need to know that those troops —" She pointed out the window. The convoy was winding its way up through the canopy of trees lining the drive. "Those troops have been taken over by enemy forces. Extraterrestrial enemy forces. We must do everything we can to stop them."

"Extraterrestrial?" MacDonald gaped at her. "Aliens? You've gotta be joking!"

<She is not joking,> Ax said, slightly offended. <My presence *should* prove that.>

MacDonald considered this. Rubbed a hand over his face. "Aliens. Okay. So what do we do?"

"The governor is our main concern right now," I said. "If we can get the Controllers, the aliens, out of here, can you keep her safe until Colonel Larsen's battalion arrives?"

"Yeah," MacDonald said. "Not a problem."

"Good." I turned to the governor. "I can't tell you where we're staying. You won't be able to contact us, but we'll contact you. Soon."

"How?" she asked.

"I'm not sure. But we'll find a way. We always do."

<We haven't thought through this superhero business very well.> Tobias flapped down from the windowsill.

MacDonald stared at him. "That bird did *not* talk," he muttered. "That bird did not talk."

Ax took the governor's hand and bowed low. <It has been an honor,> he said.

"For me, too," she replied.

I shook her hand next and held it for maybe a second too long.

The governor's head bobbed. Her chin dropped to her chest. She almost seemed to doze off while leaning against her desk. I released her hand, and she blinked herself awake.

"Oh!" She rubbed the circles under her eyes. "Guess the coffee's not working."

"Don't worry about it," I said. "It's been a long day. Okay, I need to make a quick pit stop before we leave."

I darted into the bathroom and gathered what

131

I needed. Then I strolled back into the office, my arms folded tightly across my chest.

Armstrong unbolted the office door. "All clear," he said.

Ax, Tobias, and I stepped into the hall. Nobody seemed to notice the soggy gray lump tucked under my shirt.

CHAPTER 24

I pushed the front door open and strode out onto the porch. Alone. My damp dress clung to my legs.

Hummers and National Guard trucks surrounded the governor's mansion. Soldiers in camouflage fatigues hunkered down behind the governor's well-tended shrubs, weapons drawn.

I peered out into an ocean of gun barrels. Pistols, rifles, howitzers, Dracon beams.

All pointing at me.

I steeled myself. Flashed what I hoped was an elected-official smile. "It's lovely to see the young men and women of our armed forces gathered here. However, I think —"

I shivered. It was too weird. The governor's

voice coming from my body. Then I reminded myself. The body wasn't mine, either.

It was the governor's.

I'd acquired her DNA when I shook her hand, then morphed in the hall outside her office. Now I was standing barefoot on her front porch, wearing her ragged fund-raising dress, trying to convince lunatics with automatic weapons that I was the real thing.

I cleared my throat. "As I was saying, I think we may have had a small miscommunication, because I don't have any National Guard events listed on my schedule. Could I speak to your commanding officer, please?"

The door of one of the Hummers swung open. A man in crisply pressed fatigues climbed out. He was short and tan and built like a bulldog. He strode across the drive, sunlight glinting off his spit-polished boots.

He stopped in front of me. His cold, hard eyes bored through my skull. "That's me," he said. "I'm in charge here."

"Good." I nodded. Had to keep up the act. "Well, then, Col — Capt —"

I frowned at the shiny gold eagles on his collar. What rank did that make him? Colonel? Captain? Extreme Exhaulted Emperor?

"Well, then . . . sir," I said. "I was not informed that a military exercise would be taking place on my front lawn today."

His face twisted into a sneer.

"This isn't an exercise," he said. "It's a well-orchestrated operation, and it's proceeding better than I could have dreamed. What is it the newspapers call you? Tough-minded? I thought our tough-minded governor would put up more of a fight. If I'd known it would be this easy, I wouldn't have brought so many friends." He swept one camouflaged arm toward the troops and trucks. "Seems like overkill, doesn't it?"

His lips stretched across his teeth in a cold smile.

And suddenly I knew. I was looking into the eyes of Visser One. He wasn't in the human morph he usually used, but it was him.

I forced an indignant-governor frown onto my face. I couldn't let Visser One see that I recognized him. That I knew what he was planning.

That I was anything other than the governor of this state.

"I have no idea what you're talking about," I said.

"I'm sure you don't." He turned to the troops. "Corporal!"

One of the soldiers scrambled forward. "Yes, sir."

"Would you escort our governor to her vehicle?"

"Yes, sir."

"My vehicle?" I said. "But I'm not going anywhere."

"Oh, but you are," said Visser One. He turned and strode toward the Humvee. "Someplace very special."

The corporal grabbed me by the upper arm.

"Watch it!" I started to jerk away.

Keep up the act, Marco. Keep up the act.

I took a breath. "Young man," I said, "you are hurting me."

"Really? Good." The corporal hauled me across the driveway.

The other troops began to pack up their weapons and load them into the trucks. They were getting ready to leave.

I almost smiled.

The corporal shoved me face first against a big canvas-covered transport truck. He twisted my arms behind my back and snapped handcuffs around my wrists. Two of his buddies dragged me to the back of the truck.

Visser One's Humvee rumbled past. I watched it go. Scanned the drive. Were Ax and Tobias in place? I couldn't tell.

The soldiers shoved me to the ground. The corporal pulled a rope from the back of the truck and began winding it around my ankles. He wrenched each loop tight. The rope burned into my skin.

These guys did not know how to treat a lady.

"Owwww! What is your name, son? I demand to know your name, rank, and social security number. Uh, serial number. I'm suspending your pay as of this moment. You will be brought up on charges." I glared at the three soldiers. "All of you."

"Oh, no." The corporal smirked. "Not charges!"

"I'm trembling," said one of his buddies. "Look at me, I'm all a-flutter."

Great. I got stuck with comedians. Lousy ones, too.

The corporal finished tying my ankles together. His two buddies scrambled up into the back of the truck and held the canvas open.

"I really don't understand you boys," I said. "I just don't understand what's going on here."

"Don't worry. You will." The corporal lifted me over his shoulder. "You'll understand everything real soon."

He heaved me headfirst into the back of the truck, climbed in after me, and snapped the canvas shut.

We were on our way.

CHAPTER 25

I lay on my stomach. I could see the floor, the toes of a Controller's boots, and a stack of ammunition crates in the corner.

RRRRRRRrrrrrrmmmmmmm.

The truck roared to life. Shuddered as the driver shifted gears.

RRRRRRRrrrrrrmmmmmmm.

The driver gave it gas. We lurched forward, stalled out, then lurched again.

BAM!

An ammo box banged to the floor.

"Oooooooph."

Somebody heavy landed on my back.

The driver floored it, ground the gears, and we thundered down the drive. The truck bed rattled.

The canvas sides whipped in the wind. My face thumped against the cold metal floor.

"Are these ropes and handcuffs really necessary?" I said.

I rolled to my side and swung my bound ankles around in front of me. My feet were purple and numb from lack of blood flow.

"I'm not stupid," I said. "I won't try to escape."

I rocked, trying to get into a sitting position. Fell on my face and tried again.

"I'm perfectly aware that a middle-aged, out-of-shape woman is no match for three well-trained — aah!"

I sat up.

And came face-to-face with the barrel of a rifle. The corporal and his two buddies surrounded me, M-16s aimed at my head.

"Oh, honestly," I said. "Aren't you boys going a bit overboard? As I said, I'm not in a position to — ulllmph."

The corporal stuffed the corner of a filthy duffle bag into my mouth.

"Shut up already," he said.

"Huuulph." I choked on loose threads, bits of grit, and something foul and sticky clinging to the fabric. An old Coke spill.

I glared at my captors. They could've been clones. Same haircut. Same wardrobe, camouflage fatigues and combat boots. Same sneer pasted across their faces.

The only difference was the little collar pins that showed their rank. Like Visser One's gold eagles, except these were dull black stripes. The corporal had two stripes. One of his buddies had one stripe. And the other didn't have any.

Stripeless jabbed the barrel of his M-16 in my face. "What are you looking at?"

"Ur-uuhl." I shrugged and shook my head.

We rumbled down the drive. Sunlight filtered through the trees and flickered against the canvas roof.

<They took the bait.> Tobias's thought-speak sounded strong. He was nearby. <They're all headed down the drive. Every last truck and Humvee.>

I glanced up. A jagged shadow loomed above the canvas.

Rrrrrrrrrriiiiiiip.

The roof split open.

Thummmp.

And a Hork-Bajir dropped into the back of the truck.

"Hey!" The corporal swung his rifle around.

The Hork-Bajir — Tobias — lifted his knee blade.

"AAAAAAAAAAAHHHHHHHH!"

The corporal's M-16 clattered to the bed of the truck. One Stripe dove for it.

A second Hork-Bajir — Ax — dropped through the canvas.

And pinned One Stripe's hands to the floor with his tyrannosaur feet. Ax doubled his leathery fist.

WHAP!

One Stripe was out cold.

The corporal had dropped to his knees. Now he whirled. Lunged toward the fallen rifle. Tobias seized him in one clawed hand and jerked him into a stranglehold. Blood poured from the corporal's arm.

Stripeless had been slowly inching away from the fight. Now he jammed the muzzle of his rifle into my skull. "Let him go," he told Tobias, "or the governor here gets it."

Ax and Tobias froze.

The truck jolted as the driver shifted to a lower gear. We were approaching the end of the drive.

"Are you deaf?" Stripeless screamed. "I said, LET HIM GO!"

The truck shuddered to a crawl.

I looked at Tobias. Caught his gaze and held it. Shook my head. Slowly, slightly, so Stripeless wouldn't see.

Tobias nodded. Tightened his death grip on the corporal.

"You think I'm kidding? I'm not!" Stripeless jabbed my head for emphasis. "You either let him —"

The truck lurched.

"AAH!"

Stripeless tumbled backward, slammed into an ammo box, and slumped to the bed of the truck, unconscious.

<They could all use a little nap,> said Tobias. <They're a little cranky.>

He doubled his fist.

WHAP!

The corporal dropped to the floor.

Ax and Tobias rolled the Controllers together in a heap. Then they gathered the M-16s and began hacking the barrels off with their wrist blades.

I thumped my feet on the floor. "Uh-ur-ulph."

Tobias turned. <Did you say something, Marco?>

"Uh-ur-ulph. UH. UR. ULPH!"

Ax looked at me. Tilted his head. <I believe Marco is trying to tell us that while he is extremely happy to see us, he enjoys being trussed up, and could we please not remove the filthy satchel from his mouth, as he finds it quite tasty.>

142

Oh, good. Ax picks now to finally get human sarcasm.

<Yeah.> Tobias nodded. <That's what I thought he said.>

I banged my feet again. "Uh-uhl-ur-ULUPH!"

<Okay, okay. Don't get your skirt in a wad.> Tobias pulled the duffle bag from my mouth.

"Uuuuh." I wiggled my jaw. My mouth felt like sandpaper. "Thank you. Now, can you do something about the handcuffs?"

Tobias turned me around.

WHACK.

One wrist fell free.

WHACK.

Then the other. The handcuffs clanked to the floor.

I untied my feet and helped Ax and Tobias bind the Controllers together with the rope.

I stood back. Pushed a wiry gray curl from my face and straightened my dress.

We demorphed, then remorphed. Wings. Tobias and I guarded the prisoners. Ax perched on an ammo box and played lookout.

<We are approaching a tunnel,> he said.

<Perfect.> I hopped up beside him. <Get ready.>

The back of the truck grew dark. Three mallards flew through the hole in the canvas and flapped toward home.

143

CHAPTER 26

"Hey, look, Cassie!" I said. "You're a TV star."

I pointed at the TV screen, where a wolf was leaping into a crowd of National Guard troops. The wolf growled, bared its teeth, and sank them into a burly soldier's butt.

We were back home, in Ax's scoop in the Hork-Bajir valley. We were crowded around Ax's TV, watching news footage of last night's battle.

Jake and the others — Group One — had discovered the main Yeerk headquarters for troop infestation. When the Animorphs showed up, Controllers were herding hundreds of National Guard soldiers at gunpoint toward a temporary Yeerk pool.

Jake, Rachel, Cassie, and James's group,

along with a few of Toby's finest fighters, attacked. The battle quickly became bloody and desperate, and Group One realized they were losing. Badly. But they knew they couldn't give up. They couldn't bail and let hundreds of soldiers become infested with Yeerks.

Sometime after midnight, another National Guard unit made an appearance. The colonel in charge ordered the Yeerk commander to free the uninfested troops and surrender. When the Yeerk commander didn't, the colonel and his unit attacked. Again the battle was bloody and desperate, but the colonel had seen battle before, and he knew how to win. He hadn't stopped Visser One last night. But he had definitely slowed him down.

Ax flipped from a local channel to CNN.

"Hey, go back," said Jake. "I want to see that."

Ax clicked back to the local channel. A blond reporter was interviewing a grim-looking military officer on the steps outside the governor's mansion.

"That's him." Jake pointed at the screen. "The guy who kicked butt last night."

Ax turned up the volume. The interview was almost over.

". . . thank you for that detailed account, Colonel Larsen."

"Colonel Larsen? That's the governor's guy," I said. "The one who just got back from two weeks in the desert."

The reporter turned to the camera.

"That was Lieutenant Colonel Jacob P. Larsen, the newly appointed head of our state National Guard, giving us a chilling account of last night's violent clashes within National Guard ranks. Back to you, Dave."

The camera switched to the news anchor. He flashed a TV-news-guy smile.

"Thank you, Patricia. In a related story, the governor got a bit of a scare yesterday afternoon. During a fundraiser at the Ambassador Hotel, she was kidnapped by three suspects who, witnesses say, were wearing Halloween costumes. News Channel Five brings you exclusive footage of this bizarre incident."

Dave's image was replaced by that of a limousine screeching from a parking lot, a leathery serpent head poking through the limo's roof. Then the camera switched to a scene of the governor galloping along a bridge on the back of a furry, blue, four-legged creature. A gorilla and another creature — the one with the serpent head — leaped over stalled cars and wrecked delivery trucks while police officers gave chase.

The newscast ended with footage of a helicopter explosion and a slow-mo shot of a yacht sinking into the river.

"So." Jake looked at me. "You kept it all pretty quiet, huh?"

"Hey, we were showing a little finesse there," I said.

<Yeah,> said Tobias.

"Hey, guys, quiet," said Cassie. "I want to hear this."

She leaned forward and turned up the volume. An announcer's voice blared from the TV. "We interrupt your regularly scheduled program to bring you late-breaking news from the capitol."

The picture went fuzzy for a second, then focused on Patricia, the blond reporter, talking to a plump gray-haired woman.

<It is our governor,> said Ax.

Rachel stared at the TV. "She's a woman."

"Well, yeah, she's a woman, Rachel." I glanced at Tobias. "You didn't know that?"

Rachel was too impressed with the governor to be annoyed with me. "This is so cool. The highest elected official in our state is a woman." She peered at the screen.

The camera zoomed in on the governor. Her hair was a mess, her face pale. She was wearing the same sweats she'd had on yesterday, only now they were a lot more rumpled.

But when she looked into the camera, her steady gray eyes were still bright. Still focused.

Patricia pushed a microphone into her face, and the governor began to speak.

"I won't beat around the bush," she said. "I have declared a state of emergency. I repeat: a state of emergency. This is not martial law. Our police, and even our National Guard forces, cannot be trusted." She glanced at the reporter. "The news media cannot be trusted. You may not even be able to trust your friends or your own family."

She explained about Yeerks. About how, like an invisible disease, they have been infesting and slowly taking over the population.

"I know this sounds fantastic," she said. "Like something out of Hollywood. But by now you've seen the news footage. You know what I'm telling you is true. Our state, our nation, our entire world is under attack. But we are already fighting back. I have requested help from Washington, and the president has agreed to send U.S. troops."

"U.S. troops," I said. "It's what we've wanted from the beginning. Why am I not ecstatic?"

<How can you get ecstatic about all-out global war?> Tobias said.

The governor shuffled her notes. Looked into the camera again. "This is not the time for panic," she said. "It is the time for each of us to reach into our souls and pull out the courage we may not even know we possess. Our enemy is strong. But we are stronger, because we are fighting for our lives and our freedom. For our very existence."

"Thank you, Governor." The camera switched to Patricia.

Ax clicked off the TV. We sat in silence, staring at the blank screen.

#52 The Sacrifice

The next morning, Jake gathered us together to finalize our plans.

"We could kill them all with ten or twelve thousand-pound bombs," Marco's dad amended. "In an enclosed space an explosion of even one thousand-pound bomb would have incredible magnitude. The devastation would be close to that of an atomic explosion."

Rachel nodded with satisfaction. "We'd be going seriously medieval on Yeerk butt."

"The big question is how?" Jake asked. "We talked about this before. We'd have to commit everything. Everybody. Animorphs, all of them. Hork-Bajir. Parents."

"I'm out," Cassie said hotly. "I thought that maybe . . . but I can't. And I can tell you my parents are out, too."

Rachel glared at her. "Okay, Cassie," she said

in a sarcastic-sweet tone. "So, what do you think we should do instead? Just sit here and wait for the Yeerks to find us? Or maybe we should make it real easy on them and all go hop on the train for a little swim in the Yeerk pool."

"Why do you have to be so horrible?" Cassie exploded. "You are, you know. And you get worse every day. Your own mother can't even stand you!"

I was stunned. I had never heard Cassie speak that way.

Cassie turned to walk away, but Jake grabbed her sleeve. "Cassie! Come on."

"Come on what?!" Cassie spit. "You don't knowingly take innocent life. Not if you're a decent person. Not if you're not a murderer. The goal is irrelevant. I thought you knew that, Jake, but apparently . . ."

"Apparently you decided to start making decisions for me!" Jake shouted back. "Somewhere along the line you decided that you knew what was best. For everybody. Well, guess what?"

Cassie put her hands over her ears. "Don't. Stop! Just don't. Please."

The rest of the assembled group was silent. I believe it is safe to say that none of us understood what was causing Jake and Cassie to argue so furiously.

Tears began to roll down Cassie's cheeks.

"I'm sorry," she said. "I shouldn't have done it. I don't even really know why I did it. I . . . at that moment it seemed the right thing to do. The only thing. Now, I'm just sorry. I'm sorry."

"What is she talking about?" Marco whispered.

"It was me!" Cassie shouted. "I gave the Yeerks the morphing cube. I let Tom run away with it. I stopped Jake from chasing him. From killing him. Me!"

I felt my back legs weaken slightly.

Cassie? A traitor?

It did not seem possible.

"Oh, Cassie," Eva murmured.

"You did what?" Marco said, his voice hoarse.

"Tom had it. He had the cube. The only way Jake was going to get it from him was to kill him. I couldn't let Jake do that. I couldn't. I was trying to protect him."

"You were trying to protect Jake so you basically sold out the rest of the human race?" Rachel said. Her voice was tight. The voice of controlled ferocity. Violence just barely contained.

"I'm sure she didn't think of it in those terms," Tobias said softly.

"I didn't think at all," Cassie said, her voice exhausted and full of grief. "It was more of an impulse. An instinct. Something inside just told

153

me to to let Tom take the cube. I knew . . . I knew I was making a sacrifice. That I was sacrificing so much . . . Maybe now it seems stupid. But at that moment I thought I was doing the right thing. I really did."

Rachel lifted her hand. Began to make a fist. Tobias grabbed her wrist.

And surprisingly, Jake pulled Cassie to him and embraced her.

Cassie leaned her head on his shoulder.

Jake pressed his cheek against her hair. "It's okay, Cassie," he said, his voice ragged. "I'm sorry. It's okay."

Embarrassed, I averted my eyes.

After several moments Cassie withdrew from Jake's arms and faced the rest of us. "I am so sorry. I made a mistake. A horrible mistake. I won't do it again. I won't try to decide what's right for everyone. It was arrogant and dangerous. I didn't mean it to be but it was."

Jake ran his hands through his hair. "Look. This is hard stuff. But we've got to work as a team. We don't have room for individual agendas. We go or we don't go. But either way . . ."

Jake's voice droned on. But I was not listening.

I could not stop looking at Cassie.

I was not exactly sure what I was feeling.

But it was very close to hatred.

Extinction Express!

ANIMORPHS®

K. A. Applegate

In a masterful maneuver, the Yeerks have extended their underground subway lines to run directly to the Yeerk pool, and are loading people onto the trains for mass infestation.

Ax and the Animorphs know of only one way to stop the Yeerks' subterranean assault—but it means sacrificing hundreds, maybe thousands of human lives. They've never been able to justify such brutal action before. But now that the fight is changing, it may be time for a new approach.

ANIMORPHS #52: THE SACRIFICE

Coming to Bookstores this March

Only 3 books left in the series!

Watch ANIMORPHS TV on NICKELODEON®

ANIMORPHS

K. A. Applegate

☐ BBP 0-590-62977-8	#1: The Invasion	☐ BBP 0-439-07031-7	#31: The Conspiracy
☐ BBP 0-590-62978-6	#2: The Visitor	☐ BBP 0-439-07032-5	#32: The Separation
☐ BBP 0-590-62979-4	#3: The Encounter	☐ BBP 0-439-07033-3	#33: The Illusion
☐ BBP 0-590-62980-8	#4: The Message	☐ BBP 0-439-07034-1	#34: The Prophecy
☐ BBP 0-590-62981-6	#5: The Predator	☐ BBP 0-439-07035-X	#35: The Proposal
☐ BBP 0-590-62982-4	#6: The Capture	☐ BBP 0-439-10675-3	#36: The Mutation
☐ BBP 0-590-99726-2	#7: The Stranger	☐ BBP 0-439-10676-1	#37: The Weakness
☐ BBP 0-590-99728-9	#8: The Alien	☐ BBP 0-439-10677-X	#38: The Arrival
☐ BBP 0-590-99729-7	#9: The Secret	☐ BBP 0-439-10678-8	#39: The Hidden
☐ BBP 0-590-99730-0	#10: The Android	☐ BBP 0-439-10679-6	#40: The Other
☐ BBP 0-590-99732-7	#11: The Forgotten	☐ BBP 0-439-11515-9	#41: The Familiar
☐ BBP 0-590-99734-3	#12: The Reaction	☐ BBP 0-439-11516-7	#42: The Journey
☐ BBP 0-590-49418-X	#13: The Change	☐ BBP 0-439-11517-5	#43: The Test
☐ BBP 0-590-49423-6	#14: The Unknown	☐ BBP 0-439-11518-3	#44: The Unexpected
☐ BBP 0-590-49424-4	#15: The Escape	☐ BBP 0-439-11519-1	#45: The Revelation
☐ BBP 0-590-49430-9	#16: The Warning	☐ BBP 0-439-11520-5	#46: The Deception
☐ BBP 0-590-49436-8	#17: The Underground	☐ BBP 0-439-11521-3	#47: The Resistance
☐ BBP 0-590-49441-4	#18: The Decision	☐ BBP 0-439-11522-1	#48: The Return
☐ BBP 0-590-49451-1	#19: The Departure	☐ BBP 0-439-11523-X	#49: The Diversion
☐ BBP 0-590-49637-9	#20: The Discovery	☐ BBP 0-439-11524-8	#50: The Ultimate
☐ BBP 0-590-76254-0	#21: The Threat	☐ BBP 0-439-11525-6	#51: The Absolute
☐ BBP 0-590-76255-9	#22: The Solution		
☐ BBP 0-590-76256-7	#23: The Pretender	☐ BBP 0-590-21304-0	<Megamorphs #1>:
☐ BBP 0-590-76257-5	#24: The Suspicion		The Andalite's Gift
☐ BBP 0-590-76258-3	#25: The Extreme	☐ BBP 0-590-95615-9	<Megamorphs #2>:
☐ BBP 0-590-76259-1	#26: The Attack		In the Time of Dinosaurs
☐ BBP 0-590-76260-5	#27: The Exposed	☐ BBP 0-439-06164-4	Alternamorphs:
☐ BBP 0-590-76261-3	#28: The Experiment		The First Journey
☐ BBP 0-590-76262-1	#29: The Sickness	☐ BBP 0-439-14263-6	Alternamorphs #2:
☐ BBP 0-590-76263-X	#30: The Reunion		The Next Passage

Also available:

☐ BBP 0-590-03639-4	<Megamorphs #3>: Elfangor's Secret	$5.99 US
☐ BBP 0-439-17307-8	<Megamorphs #4>: Back to Before	$5.99 US
☐ BBP 0-590-10971-5	The Andalite Chronicles	$5.99 US
☐ BBP 0-590-21798-9	The Ellimist Chronicles	$5.99 US
☐ BBP 0-439-04291-7	The Hork-Bajir Chronicles (Hardcover Edition)	$12.95 US
☐ BBP 0-439-08764-3	Visser (Hardcover Edition)	$12.95 US

Available wherever you buy books, or use this order form.

Scholastic Inc., P.O. Box 7502, Jefferson City, MO 65102

Please send me the books I have checked above. I am enclosing $_____ (please add $2.00 to cover shipping and handling). Send check or money order—no cash or C.O.D.s please.

Name_____ Birth date_____

Address_____

City_____ State/Zip_____

Please allow four to six weeks for delivery. Offer good in U.S.A. only. Sorry, mail orders are not available to residents of Canada. Prices subject to change.

ANIB301

http://www.scholastic.com/animorphs